I0781209

Wed or Dead

Cynthia Eden

HOCUS POCUS
PUBLISHING

This book is a work of fiction. Any similarities to real people, places, or events are not intentional and are purely the result of coincidence. The characters, places, and events in this story are fictional.

Published by Hocus Pocus Publishing, Inc.

Copyright © 2012, 2024 by Cindy Roussos

All rights reserved. This publication may not be reproduced, distributed, or transmitted in any form without the express written consent of the author except for the use of small quotes or excerpts used in book reviews. No part of this work may be used in the training of AI models.

If you have any problems, comments, or questions about this publication, please contact info@hocuspocuspublishing.com.

She not-so-accidentally married a wolf shifter…

Hunter Kayla Kincaid had one job—get close to wolf alpha Gage Ryder by *any means necessary*. That *means* hadn't *necessarily* included marriage, but the minute she met the shifter, Kayla began to fall under his spell. Now she's stuck between a wolf and a serious hard place. She's supposed to help take out her new husband. Instead, she's trying to find a way to save his savage self, even as Gage reveals that he's been keeping secrets of his own.

He fell for a hunter, and now she is *his*.

It's adorable the way Gage's new bride thinks that she has tricked him. Priceless. The truth is that he recognized her as a potential wolf mate from the first look, and Gage moved heaven and hell to make her his. Now that he has Kayla, there is no way Gage will let her go. So all of the hunters at the door had better back off. This wolf has his mate, and he will fight to the death in order to keep her.

WED OR DEAD was originally released in the HOWL FOR IT anthology published by Kensington in August of 2012. It contains 44,000 words, a fierce alpha hero, and a heroine who enjoys a walk on the wild side. Paranormal fun, action, and adventure are waiting. Kayla and her alpha wolf are about to show that some bonds are absolutely meant to be. Provided, of course, that they can both stay alive long enough to get their happily-ever-after.

Introduction

WED OR DEAD was originally released in the HOWL FOR IT anthology published by Kensington in August of 2012. I am thrilled to be rereleasing the title and bringing the paranormal tale to readers once again!

WED OR DEAD contains 44,000 words, a fierce alpha hero, and a heroine who enjoys a walk on the wild side. Paranormal fun, action, and adventure are waiting.

Kayla and her alpha wolf are about to show that some bonds are absolutely meant to be. Provided, of course, that they can both stay alive long enough to get their happily-ever-after.

For Megan—The OG. Thanks for giving me my start in this business. Your insight and assistance will always be appreciated! Hope you're living your best life.

Chapter One

THE BRIDE ALMOST LEFT HER GROOM AT THE ALTAR. The temptation was pretty damn strong.

Normally, Kayla Kincaid wasn't afraid of anyone or anything, but when she put one foot down on that too-red carpet at the Forever Chapel, her heart raced so fast that her chest hurt. She gripped the flowers in her hand, a small bouquet of daisies that the groom had grabbed from God knew where. There was music playing. Some sweet little old lady was nearby, stroking an organ and smiling, and Kayla realized that she had frozen after taking that single step.

This was her wedding day? How in the hell had this happened? She wasn't supposed to be getting married. She should be hightailing it out of Vegas and not getting all sweaty-palmed around the daisies as she got ready to say *I do.*

How? *How had this happened?* Her death grip tightened on the slumping bouquet.

Then the groom turned toward her and flashed that

megawatt smile of his. The smile that revealed all of his perfect, white teeth.

Oh, right. That was how.

Gage Riley waited for her at the end of that narrow aisle. The groom. She swallowed. He wasn't dressed in a fancy tux. He wore jeans that clung to his lean hips and a black T-shirt that stretched taut over his muscled chest and those wonderfully big and broad shoulders that had probably made plenty of women drool over the years.

With his perfect, sculpted face, that rock-hard jaw, his wild mane of midnight black hair, and those sky blue eyes, he was the sexiest man she'd ever seen.

She managed to unfreeze herself and take another step toward him. *Gage.* Sexy, but dangerous. Oh, she knew he was dangerous.

He was also a job. Her assignment. And Kayla had her orders.

Get close to him. By any means necessary. In this case, any means included marriage.

But...

But this didn't *feel* like an assignment.

The little old lady playing the organ began to frown at her. Gage just kept smiling. He looked confident. Strong. He had no doubt that they were about to be joined as man and wife. Kayla couldn't help glancing over her shoulder. There were about five feet between her and the front door. Maybe...maybe she should just make a run for it. Before things went past the point of no return.

She tried to swallow again. The lump in her throat was getting worse.

Warm, strong fingers curled around her arm, just below her elbow. Kayla didn't jump because she'd grown used to the silent way that Gage could move. Despite the guy's big size, he was eerily quiet when he walked, and, jeez, Gage was *fast*.

"Going somewhere?" Gage asked in the deep, dark voice that sounded like sin in the night.

Very slowly, Kayla turned her head back so that she faced him. The smile had slipped from his face. Such a handsome face. He always looked so open and almost carefree.

But there was more to Gage than met the eye. Much, much more. Her gaze dropped to his lips. Sensual. She'd felt those lips on hers plenty of times. That had been the plan, right? Get close? Make him trust her?

Only marriage hadn't been on *her* agenda. It had been on his. He'd pushed for this, and she'd realized that if she didn't take this step, she'd lose her connection to him. Then the assignment would go to hell.

"It's too late to run," he told her. His hand lifted and brushed against her cheek. The caress was gentle. So at odds with the fierce strength that she knew he could wield. "I'd just follow you, sweetheart."

She was killing the daisies. The little old lady had stopped playing and was now glaring at her in a not-so-sweet way. The minister—wait, was he a minister or a justice of the peace—or something else? Whatever. The man peered suspiciously at them from his perch near the front of the chapel.

Gage leaned toward her and his lips pressed lightly against hers. "It's just a few simple words. Nothing for you to be afraid of."

Kayla stiffened. "I'm not afraid." Admitting fear to herself was one thing. Confessing it out loud, to someone else? *No way.*

Besides, she wasn't *really* afraid. Nervous. That was all.

A wee bit nervous. Gage was the one who should be afraid. He didn't know just what he was setting himself up for here.

He didn't know her. Not really.

If he did, he would be the one running.

Her groom-to-be had no idea that she'd stashed a gun in her purse. Or that she kept a knife—*silver*—strapped to her ankle. He didn't know that she'd spent most of her adult life becoming a perfect predator, and he damn sure didn't know that he was her current prey.

Gage's lips caressed hers once more in a light kiss even as he pulled the damaged daisies from her hand. When his head lifted, his blue eyes seemed even brighter. "Good. If you're not afraid, then come marry me." A thread of demand underscored the words.

Gage wasn't usually the demanding sort. He was more easygoing, more—

He tossed the daisies on a nearby chair and threaded his fingers through hers. "Want me to carry you?" His smile flashed again.

That smile of his was like her freaking kryptonite. No man should have a smile that melted panties. His did.

The organ began to play again. *One foot in front of the other.* Kayla took a deep breath and began to walk. *One foot.*

Gage was right by her side.

In front of the other.

Before she knew it, they were standing at the front of the chapel. The officiant smiled as the light reflected off the top of his bald head. He was talking. Nodding. Looking all pleased and happy.

Kayla couldn't hear a word he said. Her heart raced too fast and too loud for that.

Gage kept a tight hold on her hand. Probably because he was afraid she'd make a break for it.

But Kayla wasn't leaving. She'd never left a job before, and she wouldn't start now. From the corner of her eye, she glanced at Gage. Poor guy. He had no idea what was coming for him. Did he think this was some kind of epic romance?

Think again.

She was the predator. He was the prey. And, soon enough, he'd grow to hate her.

Gage nudged her. When she glanced up and found the officiant staring at her, Kayla realized she was supposed to speak. "Uh, I do." That was what folks always said, right? *Promise to love, honor, and cherish.*

But what she'd really do...*Lie, betray, and hurt.*

Her chest began to ache. This wasn't what she wanted. Why couldn't things have been simpler for her? For him?

The officiant beamed. Gage's strong voice rumbled beside her as he made his vow.

And she hated her life. Just once, she wished she could be normal. A woman in love—a woman actually marrying the man of her dreams. Instead of just being a woman who was using herself as bait to set up her groom.

Gage turned her toward him. Even over the too-loud thud of her heartbeat, Kayla heard the officiant say that Gage could kiss his wife.

"Hello, wife," Gage murmured, and finally—*finally*—the wild drumming of her heartbeat quieted, because it stopped for a few seconds. "You're mine, now. Forever." The words held a hard edge that she'd never heard before in his voice.

Then Gage kissed her. Not the light, teasing kisses that

he'd given her in the past. An openmouthed, hot, I-want-you-naked kiss that sent a shudder through her whole body.

She kissed him back just as wildly. Because despite all the other madness that was happening, Kayla did want her husband. And, before he found out the truth about her and this little fantasy came to a crashing end, she'd have him.

* * *

THE HOTEL ROOM was one of those ridiculous pink explosions that you found in Vegas. A romance-ready room. Heart-shaped Jacuzzi. Rose petals scattered on the floor and on the massive bed. Pink champagne chilling next to a box of chocolates on the bedside table.

But when Gage carried Kayla inside the decked out room, his bride didn't so much as give the surroundings a glance. Her eyes—big, golden, fuck-me eyes—were on him. Her hands curled around his neck. "I want you." Her soft confession.

Did she actually sound a little surprised by that fact?

Damn, sometimes, she was so adorable...he could just eat her. Actually, he would.

He couldn't believe that he'd gotten her to marry him. The lady had sure surprised him on that one. He'd been expecting her to run as fast as she could.

But she'd straightened her slim shoulders. Lifted her slightly pointed chin. And let him drag her down the aisle.

A surprise, but he wouldn't question fate. Not then.

Gage kicked the hotel room door closed and carried Kayla to the bed. He'd been wanting to get her naked and beneath him since the first night they met. Now that he had her in that room with him, nothing was going to stop him from claiming her.

Except...

Kayla put her hand on his chest when he closed in on her. Gage was leaning over the bed, more than ready to taste her, when her small hand slammed into his chest.

"I ...ah...need a minute."

Seriously? She'd put him off for weeks. Tempting him with that sweet ass and those gorgeous breasts, and now that she was legally *his,* the woman was still putting the brakes on things?

He barely bit back a growl. A man's control could last only so long.

But he pulled away. Stood. Began to strip.

Her eyes widened as she looked at his chest, and her pink tongue slipped out to lick along her plump lower lip. He had plans for that tongue. And for her.

Sexy little Kayla Kincaid. The first time he'd seen her, he'd gotten hard and territorial. One look, and he'd thought...*mine.*

Sometimes, you knew what you wanted with one glance.

She eased onto her feet. Stood beside him a moment. The top of her head barely skimmed his shoulders. Her dark hair—silky, curling lightly—drifted down her back as she tilted her head to stare up at him. "I'll be right back," she promised.

His gaze dropped to her lips. Full, red. Bitable. Just like the rest of her.

He did like to bite.

Kayla turned away and darted into the bathroom. *Hurry back, sweetheart.*

His control wasn't lasting much longer.

He wanted her in that bed. Wanted her spread wide. And he wanted to hear her scream his name.

For almost two months, he'd played her game. Done the whirlwind courtship bit. Acted like the gentleman for her. Wore a mask to hide the real way he felt. The real way he *was*.

Playtime was over.

Kayla had her secrets. So did he. The time for a big reveal would come later. The time for fucking—yeah, that was *now*.

The bathroom door squeaked open. Gage turned to face her, still clad in his jeans. His eyes went to her face first. Heart-shaped, delicate—deceptively so. Her eyes were shining, her high cheeks flushed, and she looked—

Excited. Gorgeous.

And naked.

His gaze swept down her body and the cock that was already up for her hardened even more against the zipper of his jeans.

Her breasts were small, but rounded perfectly with light pink nipples that he couldn't wait to have against his tongue. Her hips curved, flaring, and the sight of her parted thighs had his mouth going dry.

Take her.

He'd waited long enough.

"Why are you still dressed?" Kayla wanted to know. He managed to drag his gaze away—okay, on the third attempt, he dragged it away from her pert breasts—and back up to her face. "I thought you were supposed to be stripping."

He nearly ripped his jeans off. Then in one lunge, he was at her side. Gage lifted her up, holding her easily, and he thrust his tongue into her mouth. Her arms wrapped around him—and so did her legs. Her soft, hot sex brushed against his cock even as her tight nipples pushed against his chest.

He was gonna go freaking insane. Gage wasn't a man accustomed to waiting, but for her, he'd tried. *Can't wait longer.* Because he could smell the lush scent of her arousal. She wanted him. He was on fire for her.

His tongue met hers. Tasted. She was always a blend of sweet and spicy on his tongue. Innocence and sin. Such a mixed combination. One that fit her too well.

He pulled his mouth from hers and began to kiss a path down her neck. He was strong. Gage doubted that she understood just how powerful he really was, and he easily kept her lifted against him.

When his tongue licked over her skin, down low where her shoulder curved into her neck, Kayla shivered.

He'd make her do more than that.

His teeth scored her flesh. Bit lightly. Marked her. That was the way of his kind.

Her nails dug into his shoulders. Her breath came in ragged pants, and Gage could feel the slick wetness of her core against him. *More.*

He'd known she'd be like this. White-hot to the touch. Able to burn a man straight to the soul.

He lifted her higher and her soft gasp would have made him smile, if he hadn't been so damn hungry for her. But there were no smiles now. No soft touches or kisses. There was only lust, blazing out of control.

He held her in the perfect position for his mouth, and he took her breast between his lips. He licked, sucked, and her breaths came even faster. His cock was so swollen it hurt, and he wanted to drive into her more than he'd ever wanted anything else.

"*Gage!*"

No, actually, he did want something else. He wanted her to come for him.

Still holding her, he headed for the bed. He lowered her onto the covers and rose petals slid beneath her. Their light fragrance mixed with the sweet scent that was just *Kayla*.

She was making him crazy.

Gage took his time licking and tasting her other breast. Her hands were on him. Her fingers slid over his back and urged him closer.

Not yet.

Kayla's legs were parted, and he stood between them at the side of the bed. The perfect position to thrust deep, if he'd wanted to thrust.

Not yet.

He wanted another taste. A far more intimate one.

His gaze dipped to her sex and her legs widened even more. "Do you know..." His voice was so dark he knew it sounded more like a growl than anything else. "Do you know how long I've wanted to put my mouth on you?"

Her lashes lifted. She stared back at him with glinting eyes and flushed cheeks. Then Kayla shook her head. He saw the flash of hesitation in her gaze, the innocence that he'd learned could appear and vanish in an instant. She tried to come off so tough and assured, but that innocence kept slipping out.

His knees hit the carpet as he lowered his body between her splayed legs. Gage wrapped his hands around her hips and pulled her to the edge of the mattress so that her thighs brushed against either side of his shoulders. "Since the first night, you came into the bar"—*his* bar—"wearing that short black skirt, and I kept wondering if you had on anything underneath it." He'd looked at her and gotten hard. Wanted. Craved. "And I wanted to shove that skirt up..." Gage put his hands between her thighs and loved her gasp. "And find out."

Her eyes were on him. So wide. So deep.

He'd been insane for her. The need always pulsing in his body, but Kayla hadn't let him get close enough to fuck. Not that first night. Not all the nights since. They'd danced around each other for weeks, becoming closer and closer, but deep kisses and heavy petting had been all that he'd gotten from her.

Until tonight. Until they'd drank until one a.m. at his bar, then slipped out to find a chapel.

Now he had her. There'd be no escape for her. Or him.

His fingers slid into her. She was wet and tight. Perfect.

But he didn't just want to touch with his fingers. He licked his lips, then Gage put his mouth on her. Her hips bucked up against him as she gasped out his name, but his left hand just rose again and locked around her hip, holding her easily in place.

He let his tongue slide over her sex. Sweet, slick, and delicious. Hot. He used the fingers of his right hand to open her to him. To press lightly into her even as his tongue raked over her clit.

She wasn't trying to pull away anymore. Kayla was pushing against him, and her body was eager for more. Fair enough, he was more than eager, too.

He devoured her. Gage's mouth took and tasted even as his fingers thrust into her. She moaned and shivered and her body tightened beneath him.

He wanted her to come against his mouth. Then she'd be ready for him. He didn't want to hurt her the first time, so he *had* to make sure she was ready for him.

And her taste...*sweet and rich.* Better than the most decadent of chocolates. And decadent chocolate had always been his vice.

One of them, anyway. He had quite a few.

He pulled his fingers back and thrust his tongue into her. His thumb pushed down on the center of her need and she came, jerking beneath him.

Gage pulled back, savored her taste on his tongue, and knew that he now had a new vice. *Her.* The lady was at the top of his list.

He'd have more of her. All of her. *Now.* He reached over and yanked out one of the condoms that waited inside the nightstand. Part of the romance package. The hotel knew how to please its guests. He was about to be pretty fucking pleased.

Because he was finally having her.

He donned the condom, and two seconds later, his cock pushed against the entrance to her body. Her eyes were on him. He couldn't go easy anymore. He'd used the last of his control. But she was ready now. She had to be.

Kayla arched against him, and Gage thrust balls-deep into her core. A ragged groan ripped from him because she felt so good. Tight. Wet. Hot.

He pulled back, but her sex clamped around him, gripping like a fist along the length of his cock.

So good.

Her eyes were open and on him. "Give me more," she whispered.

And he did. Gage drove into her, deep and hard, and the bed squeaked beneath them. Rose petals were going everywhere, and he didn't give a damn. All that mattered was taking her. Claiming her.

In and out. He thrust again and again. Her legs wrapped round him, holding him tightly. Her nipples stabbed up into the air, and he just had to taste one again. He leaned forward and took one pebbled nipple into his mouth.

Her fingers sank into his hair. "Gage!" Her inner muscles tightened even more around him as her body stiffened. Her second climax was close. Hell, *yes*.

His head lifted because he wanted to watch her come. One thrust. Another. Then her lips parted as she called out his name. Pleasure flooded over her features. Her eyes lit with golden fire. Her cheeks flushed an even darker pink.

And she came around his cock.

Gage exploded inside of her, letting his own release pump through him. The pleasure nearly ripped him apart, pulsing in his blood and giving him a heady rush that had Gage clenching his teeth and holding her even tighter.

This, this was beyond just sex. Beyond the fleeting pleasure he'd known with other women. This was fucking fantastic.

Gage leaned forward and pressed a soft kiss to her lips.

Kayla jumped, as if she was startled by that gentle touch, and her eyes widened as she looked at him. "That was..." She licked her lips. "It—"

"It was the start," he told her, smiling, and getting hard within her again. *Need another condom.* Good thing that box in the drawer was full. "And, sweetheart, the pleasure is only gonna get better." He'd guarantee it.

He'd finally gotten Kayla exactly where he wanted her —and Gage wasn't going to let her go.

So he put his mouth back on her delectable body. This time, he skimmed his lips over the raised scars that slid over her shoulder, and he knew that the night was going to be incredible.

* * *

THE FAINT LIGHT of dawn slipped through the curtains when Kayla eased from the bed. Gage still lay tangled amid the covers, and his dark lashes cast shadows on his cheeks. Unable to help herself, she paused and just stared down at him for a moment.

He looked so peaceful. The lines were smoothed from his face. The wild power of his eyes was shielded by his lowered lids.

Just a man. That was what he looked like then. With his tanned skin appearing even darker against the crisp, white sheets, with a rose petal in his hair—he just looked like a man.

Not a monster.

She turned away and crept toward the bathroom.

He was a man, and she was supposed to just be a woman.

If only. Life sure had a way of sucking.

Kayla shut the door behind herself. After taking a deep breath, she glanced up and stared at the reflection in the mirror. Her lips were swollen. Her eyes glittering. Her hair was an insane tangle around her face. She didn't know how many times she'd climaxed, but she did know that Gage was the best lover she'd ever had.

Yep, he was at the top of her big list of four men. She figured he'd be staying at the top for a very long while.

She straightened her shoulders. There were some faint red marks on her neck. Marks that Gage had left. She'd left her own share of marks on him, too. They'd been wild. Fierce.

Happy.

Just like a real honeymooning couple.

She glanced away from the mirror, almost hating the

sight of her own reflection. *Why couldn't it have all been true?*

Because her life wasn't a fairy tale. She wasn't some princess who got to live happily-freaking-after in a castle.

I've always been more the wicked queen type.

And Gage wasn't Prince Charming, no matter how tempting he appeared to be.

Kayla reached for the handbag she'd put in the bathroom hours before. The bag, her clothes, and her weapons. It was almost six a.m. Just minutes away. That meant her call would be coming in three, two, one—

Kayla answered the phone before it could even fully vibrate in her hand. "The job is done," she told her boss. The job. Her marriage. Getting close to Gage Riley. She'd done everything she was supposed to do.

"Not quite," came the rumble of Lyle McKennis's voice. "But you're real close, Kincaid."

Her hands tightened around the phone. Close wasn't good enough. Close wasn't—

"Actually, you're killing close," he continued, voice cold and flat in her ear. "You're the only hunter who's ever been able to slide under Riley's radar."

Because when Gage Riley saw her, he saw just a woman. Not a hunter.

"You know what he's done," Lyle said. "You know what he is."

Yes. She looked up and forced herself to stare into the mirror again. She stared past her own reflection. Gazed at those marks on her neck.

"He's sleeping now, isn't he?" Lyle murmured.

"Yes." Why was her body starting to feel so cold? Numb?

"Then it's time." Satisfaction purred through Lyle's words. "Make sure you use silver."

What other weapon would she use? Nothing else would work, not on Gage.

"Go kill your new husband," Lyle ordered, "and give the world one less monster to fear."

Chapter Two

THE KNIFE WAS A LIGHT WEIGHT IN HER HAND. SHE'D killed before with a weapon like this one, and Kayla had no doubt that she'd do so again. But...

Killing Gage? Ice seemed to fill her veins.

Yes, she knew that had been Lyle's plan all along. From the first moment, when he'd told her to head into Gage's bar and to charm her way into Gage's world. She'd known Lyle wanted her to take out Gage. Another target. Another mission.

She'd always been such a good soldier. No, *hunter.*

Only the plan had changed for her. Gage was supposed to be a monster, she *knew* that. Lyle had told her all about Gage's crimes. She'd read his file. Read it over a dozen times.

But when she looked at him, she didn't see the monster. She just saw the man.

A man who'd wanted to marry her.

So on her thirty-fourth birthday, she'd headed to the chapel with him. And now, with dawn coming, the game was supposed to be over.

She was killing close. Lyle had that bit right. Gage trusted her. This was the time her group had been waiting for. They'd planned this attack for months.

Carefully, she opened the bathroom door. The door made just the softest of creaks as it slid over the carpet. Gage still slept in bed, but he'd rolled so that his back was to her. Such a strong, muscled back. There were faint scars on his back. She'd touched them in the dark. Just as he'd touched her scars.

He'd kissed her scars. The lines that sliced over her skin. He hadn't asked her about them. Hadn't questioned like her other lovers had done. He'd just stroked them with his fingers and his tongue and made her feel perfect.

She'd never been that.

Kayla glanced at the knife. Was she really supposed to just shove it into his heart? Then walk away while he bled out?

You know what he is. Don't be fooled. Gage's kind was so good at deception. She had to remember that. He'd been born to lie. To deceive.

She'd met others like him before. So many over the years. More than most people realized.

Her own family had been attacked by someone like Gage long ago. A man, hiding a beast inside. One dark night, he'd killed her mother and father. Left her brother in a pool of blood, struggling to breathe. Attacked her.

Monsters lived and breathed in this world. Most folks didn't know that truth. They thought the world was all happy and shiny and full of birthday parties, play dates, and football games.

She knew better. *Monsters are real.* And her handsome husband, with his slow smile and strong hands—he was a monster.

Kayla took a step forward. *One foot in front of the other.* The mantra was the same one she'd used when she'd walked down the aisle. Only no beaming wedding official waited for her this time.

The robe she wore rustled around her legs as she took another slow step. Another.

When she felt something wet on her cheek, Kayla stopped. What the hell? Her left hand lifted and swiped across her face. Was she crying? She *never* cried. She hadn't, not since the men at the cemetery had put her parents in the ground.

"Come back to bed," Gage said, his voice rumbling out and making her jump. He faced the window, not her as he added, "I miss you."

He wouldn't miss her for long.

Kayla took a deep breath and forced herself to keep walking. A few more steps, and her legs brushed against the edge of the bed. "Th-there's something you should know about me." His back was still to her. Why did he have to make such an easy target?

Having his back to you should make it better. You don't have to look him in the eyes when you attack.

But stabbing a man in the back had never been her style.

Liar. The insidious whisper came from deep within. Her secret shame.

Her hand clenched around the knife's handle. Gage was supposed to be dangerous. Lethal. The strongest paranormal badass to claim Vegas in years.

Because he *was* a paranormal. The supernaturals were real and breathing, and many were hiding in the shadows of Sin City.

He was the perfect target right then. Tousled hair.

Sated male. Defenseless. It would be so easy. Just lift the knife. Drive the blade into him.

"Oh, I think I already know all the secrets you have, sweetheart," he murmured, his voice a low and sexy growl.

Kayla shook her head. Damn tears. "No, you don't—"

In a flash, he rolled toward her. He leapt up and came at her with claws ripping from his fingers.

Not defenseless.

Claws...because Gage Riley wasn't human.

Shifter.

His blue eyes shined at her with the light of the beast, and he put those too-sharp and too-long claws of his at her throat.

The move actually seemed only fair, considering that she had her knife pressed over his heart.

"Hello, hunter," Gage whispered.

Her own heart shoved hard against her chest. "How long..." Kayla licked her lips. Why was her mouth so dry? "How long have you known?"

He brought his head in close to hers. Inhaled her scent. Pressed a light kiss to her cheek. Did he taste the salt of her tears? "Since the first time you walked into my bar."

What? Kayla shook her head, lost, confused. He'd known since then, and he'd still married her? Still fucked her?

His claws skated lightly over her throat. He didn't break the skin. Didn't hurt her. But she knew one slice would cut open her jugular.

"Are you really going to kill me now?" Gage asked as he pulled back to study her with a cocked head. "Just hours after our wedding?"

She was supposed to.

That was her *job.* As a hunter, she was the one sent out

to keep the humans safe in this world. When a supernatural crossed the line and started killing, her team was sent in. They delivered justice. They were the heroes.

Only she didn't feel like any kind of hero.

She felt like a killer.

"Was screwing me part of the deal?" Gage demanded as his voice roughened even more.

Her eyes narrowed at that insulting question. Maybe it was deserved, and maybe it damn well wasn't. Instead of stabbing him, she wanted to punch him.

"If so," Gage continued with a shake of his head, "that was a rather fatal mistake."

They were at a supernatural standoff. Claws versus silver. If he'd just sheathe his claws...

"Because now that I've had you,,," Gage smiled at her, and revealed his growing canines. *Sharp*. "I think I want another bite."

He'd kept his fangs from her. Kept the claws away last night. But it looked like he was done playing nice.

So was she.

The bed was rumpled. The air smelled of sex. He was naked.

She stared into his eyes. If he knew what she was, then Kayla had no idea why he'd married her. Sure, she'd been ordered to say the "I do" bit. She'd been told to do anything necessary in order to get past his defenses.

Gage Riley ran the wolf pack in Vegas. Since the wolves had moved to town just eight months ago, hell had hit the city. Supernatural madness. Attacks. Killings.

The pack had to be stopped. *By any means necessary*.

But sex wasn't a means. Making love was more. Far more.

"Lower your claws," she told him and managed to keep

her voice totally calm. Rather impressive under the circumstances, but she'd been trained to be cold. Passionless. *I'm not that way with him.* "You aren't going to kill me." Those words were the truth because she'd learned a few things about Gage during their time together.

More than a few.

He wasn't a heartless bastard. Not a cold-blooded killer.

I won't be wrong about him.

His gaze hardened as he studied her. Then the half-smile that had always charmed her curled his lips. "Killing you isn't what I have planned at all."

He dropped his claws and there still wasn't so much as a scratch on her skin.

Gage glanced down at his chest. She'd nicked him with the blade, and drops of blood trailed over his skin. Blood—and the faintest plume of smoke.

The old legend was true. Werewolves—or, in this case, wolf shifters—and silver just didn't mix.

"Now are you gonna cut my heart out?" he asked and his smile hardened. "Though to confess, sweetheart, it sure feels like you already have."

Her lips parted in surprise. Wait, what? Did he mean—

But then Gage's head jerked up. His nostrils flared, and she knew the wolf was pulling in scents. *"Company."* A snarl. His eyes had never looked so cold before. A chill skated over her. "Guess that's your backup, huh?"

No. She wasn't supposed to have any backup. Not yet. And she couldn't hear anything.

But Gage had a shifter's sense of smell and hearing. Far, far more advanced than a human's. That was why it was so hard to take out shifters. They always saw their enemies coming or smelled them. You couldn't sneak up on prey that could hear you from a mile away.

"I won't go down easy," he promised, and she believed him. It would be a bloodbath for whoever came in that door.

Kayla shook her head and dropped the knife. It fell to the carpet without making a sound. "You won't go down at all." She'd be punished for this. No question about that

But I won't kill him.

Sometimes even a hunter had to break the rules. Especially when she'd started to go soft for her prey.

Kayla turned away from him. If more of her team members really were heading down that hallway just beyond their hotel room door—and why hadn't Lyle told her that he was sending in a team so soon?—then Gage would have to act fast. "We're three floors up, but that shouldn't be an issue for you." Shifters could easily survive a fall from that height. He could jump out of the window and vanish. Simple. With dawn just breaking, there wouldn't be too many folks out to see him, and if any did, they'd just think they were having some kind of hung-over delusion in Vegas. "Go now, before they arrive."

She dropped her robe. Jerked on her own clothes. She wouldn't be naked when her team swarmed. Swarmed—and took her into custody because she'd sided with the enemy.

An enemy who attacked your own family.

Kayla yanked on her boots. She could hear the careful tread of footsteps in the hallway now, and her gut clenched.

What would happen to her? Those who disobeyed Lyle didn't exactly get the chance to hang around the unit for long and make amends. There weren't any second chances for hunters. Lyle sure didn't believe in them.

If Lyle cast her out of the unit, what would happen to her brother?

Kayla glanced around the room with its trampled rose

petals. She needed to get the silver knife and strap it back to her ankle. She had to have her weapon close by in case—

"Looking for this?" Gage drawled and the faint hint of Texas she'd heard a few times before slipped into his voice again.

Gage had dressed, but he sure hadn't fled yet. The window waited behind him, just begging for the man to leap through it and get the hell out of there. But, no, he was just standing near the wrecked bed and waving her knife between his claws.

"Go," she gritted out. In about thirty seconds, maybe less, the team would be breaking down the door. She knew their MO. They would have already cleared the third floor. Gotten all the nearby guests relocated during the night.

While I was making love to Gage.

Oh, hell, had the team heard them making love?

She hoped the walls were thicker than they looked. She hadn't exactly been playing it quiet last night. Gage had made her scream.

She'd made him growl. Maybe roar.

The silver knife was blistering his fingers. She could see the smoke from across the room. The more powerful a wolf shifter was, the more the silver was supposed to burn. If that old legend was true, Gage had to be very, very powerful, indeed.

"You think I'm gonna leave you?" Gage asked, and he threw the knife. It flashed, tumbling end over end, before embedding hilt-deep in the bed's headboard. Her gaze darted to the shaking knife handle, then back to him. Gage lifted one brow at her. "Think again."

"It will be your funeral," she whispered. Why couldn't he leave? She was trying to *help* him. Didn't he get that?

She didn't want him hurt. Kayla wanted him to have a chance.

A chance the guy wasn't taking. Dammit. Fine. Whatever. Maybe she could buy him some more time so that he could get his sanity back and flee like a smart shifter.

She turned and headed for the hotel room door. Took two fast steps.

And she was jerked back against her husband's hard, muscled body. "You're not leaving me," he told her, his words whispered right into her ear. "You promised forever, remember?"

He'd obviously gone insane. Kayla jerked against him, but there was no give to the shifter at all. She'd always known he was much stronger than he looked, but Gage's arms wouldn't budge no matter how much she twisted and shoved against him.

Then the hotel room door flew inward, driven by a powerful kick, and three men dressed in black, from toe to ski mask-covered heads, burst into the room. They were all armed, and their weapons were pointed right at—

Me.

Shit. Kayla gulped and stopped struggling.

Gage had pulled her in front of him, and he was using her as a human shield. His claws were back at her neck. *Again with that?* And a growl rumbled from his throat. Her husband was definitely showing the beast-like tendencies that he'd kept so carefully hidden for weeks.

He sure wasn't so easygoing any longer.

"Stand the hell down," Gage ordered, voice cold and deadly, "or watch her die."

The masked man in front lifted his left hand immediately in a signal she knew meant the others should freeze. She couldn't see the hunter's face, but she didn't have to. She'd know Jonah anyplace. The tall build, the wiry strength. He was the lead on this mission, and the others would do whatever he commanded.

"Let her go," Jonah said, and his own voice matched Gage's in arctic chill. The perfect hunter. Cold and emotionless. Jonah hadn't always been like that.

But then again, she hadn't always been a killer, either. They'd both been more, before.

Before a night of blood and screams. Death and hell. And monsters.

"Let her go?" Gage repeated, sounding surprised. He actually laughed, then said, "I don't think so," as he began to back up—with her still clutched tightly against him. His slow, deliberate steps eased them across the room.

Oh, so *now* he was heading toward the window? Kayla kept her movements timed with his and made sure to use her body to shield him as much as possible. At least he was fleeing now. Better late than never. He'd drop her before he made his exit. He'd be safe. She'd be—

Um, well, something.

Jonah took a step forward.

Gage's hold tightened on her. "Move again," he told the masked intruders, "and you'll find yourself walking in her blood."

Kayla's breath froze in her lungs. Were the vicious words an idle threat or the real deal? In that moment, she wasn't sure. Claws were at her throat. A shifter at her back. And guns waited in front of her.

Hardly the perfect morning-after that most brides experienced.

Jonah holstered his weapon. He gave a quick hand-motion to the two silent men behind him. They lowered their weapons.

"Why isn't he dead?" Jonah asked her.

Did he really want her to go into that *now?*

Gage stopped the backward walk they were doing. He lifted his hand and slammed it into the window. Glass shattered and rained down around their feet. Wow. Shifter strength. Humans would never be able to break the reinforced glass so easily.

"I'm not dead because she loves me," Gage told him, voice clear and loud. And definitely with a *duh* edge. "And that's why she's leaving you assholes behind and joining *me.* "

Kayla's jaw dropped, but before she could speak, Gage spun her around and pulled her flush against his body.

"Put your arms around me," he ordered with glinting eyes and a locked jaw. "And hold the hell on."

She put her arms around him but shook her head. No, he couldn't mean to take her with him. Not *through* the window. While he'd easily survive the fall and quickly heal from any broken bones, she wouldn't. As a human, she didn't have that amazing healing luxury. A fall from the third floor could kill her.

Probably *would* kill her.

Gage brought his head in close to hers. His lips feathered over her cheek, and he whispered, "Trust me, I'll keep you safe."

On a three-story fall? The hell, no, he—

Gage leapt through the remnant of the window, holding her tight, and Kayla screamed.

Wind whipped past her. *I'm dying.* So this was the way she was going out. Better than getting slashed apart by a vamp or incinerated by a demon but—

They were on the ground. Gage's knees had barely buckled. And...she was fine. Still held tightly in his arms.

No bruises. No cuts. Nothing.

Holy hell. They'd made it.

"Come on," he muttered and put her on her feet. His hand still retained a tight grip on her arm, and as he rushed forward, he hauled her behind him. Her boots crunched over the glass that had fallen from their window.

Cat shifters were supposed to be pretty freaking awesome at landing on their feet after jumps like that, but the wolf had shown her just how agile his beast could be.

"*Kayla!*" Jonah's scream had her turning back. He was leaning out of the window, and he'd jerked off his ski mask. His face was white. His eyes wild.

"I'm okay!" Kayla yelled back to him. "I'm—"

Gage grabbed her and threw her over his shoulder. Really, that was too much. No, the jump through the window had been *too* much. In a minute, she was gonna get pissed.

But she didn't have a minute. Before she could do more than pound her fist frantically into Gage's back, he tossed her inside an SUV.

Kayla could have jumped out. When he ran around to the driver's side, she could have leapt for safety. If she'd wanted safety.

But she didn't move.

And, technically, she *could* have gotten away from the guy when he first tossed her over his shoulder. Her body was a lethal weapon, after all. Not much could subdue her.

But she hadn't fought back too hard then.

She wasn't fighting now, either.

Gage jumped behind the driver's seat. He bent low and hot-wired the ride. *Sneaky and impressive.* She liked a man with skills. Then he gunned the engine as he shot the SUV out of the parking lot fast enough to make her head whip back.

They'd be pursued, she knew that. Lyle wouldn't just let them vanish into the night.

No way would he do that. The real hunt...well, it was only getting started.

Chapter Three

As a rule, Gage was good at losing any tails who thought they were dumb enough to be able to track him.

This wasn't his first life-or-death ball game. Not even close. So he raced through the city, cutting down side streets, twisting the SUV through tight alleys, and taking all the shortcuts that most wouldn't know about in Vegas.

He switched vehicles at a run-down gas station. When they ditched the SUV for a pickup, Kayla didn't even try to run from him. Huh. She wasn't talking, but she wasn't running, either. Was that a good sign?

He wasn't sure quite what to make of it. Or her.

So he just kept heading toward the desert. Dust trailed behind them, and in his rearview mirror, he saw nothing but an open road.

No tail. No more hunters.

It looked as if they'd gotten away clean. For the moment.

Gage exhaled slowly and some of the battle-ready tension started to ease from him. The beast who'd wanted to claw his way to freedom stopped fighting the leash Gage had wrapped around the wolf's neck.

"You're not just gonna dump me in the desert, are you?" Ah, his wife finally spoke. Pity her words just pissed him off.

Is that who she thinks I am? What I am? A killer. His hands clenched around the wheel. "I've got other plans for you."

She took that in silence, and anger churned higher in him. He wanted Kayla to strike back at him. To yell. To explode. But she didn't.

Kayla simply sat there, looking too sexy and fuckable, with her hair mussed and her head turned away as she glanced out at the blurring terrain. Her profile gave no hint of her emotions, but she had to be feeling something. He was about to rip apart inside.

Stick to the plan. Stick. To. It.

He'd known all along that she had secrets. The fact that was she was a hunter—

"I let you escape."

He laughed at her confession. Such bullshit. Did she even see it? "Sweetheart, I let myself escape." That was why he'd booked a room on the third floor. That kind of jump was nothing to him. Always have an exit strategy—that was his motto.

Always.

He jerked the wheel to the right and barreled down the thin strip of road that most folks would never even notice, not the way it was nestled behind an old, run-down highway billboard.

From the corner of his eye, he saw Kayla stiffen. "Where are we going?" Now there was suspicion in her tone.

Because she realized that he wasn't just blindly fleeing the city, scared of the big, old tough hunters.

Fuck that. No, fuck them. He'd never been afraid of hunters, and he wouldn't start now. He'd left Vegas for a reason.

In less time than it took to shift, he could have taken out every man in that hotel room. He hadn't, though, because that wouldn't have been part of his plan—and he did have a plan.

So now it was his turn to play the silent game. But the game didn't last long. All too soon, they were pulling up next to the small, wooden cabin that lay nestled in the middle of freaking nowhere.

Before he'd even parked, two men strode toward them. One was tall, fair, with light hair. The other—dark-haired and leaner—shadowed the blond's movements. Neither man looked particularly happy.

What else was new?

Gage almost smiled. He would have, if he hadn't still been so pissed off. *She'd betrayed him.*

He jumped from the truck and slammed the door shut behind him.

The blond approached. "Thought you'd be here sooner," Davis Black said, rubbing his chin as he surveyed the pack alpha.

"Um..." This came from the other wolf shifter. A grin lifted his lips as William "Billy" Tanner glanced over Gage's shoulder and back at the truck. "Trouble with the missus?" The light hint of his native Mississippi drawl rolled beneath Billy's voice.

Gage narrowed his eyes. "Nothing I can't handle." The other members of the pack wouldn't be making an appearance. That was the plan. Only his top two enforcers were supposed to meet him here.

The others would wait, until he needed them.

"Is everything set up?" Gage asked as his gaze swept the area. The place looked deserted. With its sagging roof and busted windows, the cabin seemed damn near uninhabitable. But appearances could be deceiving.

Why didn't humans ever seem to truly understand that fact?

The truck door squeaked behind him. So Kayla was coming after him now?

Control. He just had to hold on for a little longer. A few more minutes, and he'd have her in the cabin. They'd be alone. Just a few more—

He saw Billy's nostrils flare. "Oh, man, she smells *good*. Like sex and—"

His control snapped, and Gage slammed his fist into Billy's jaw. Though he was stronger than a human, Billy wasn't an alpha, and that blow had him stumbling back.

"Billy," Gage barked out as the wolf howled inside of him, "don't push me right now." The thread of his control had been stripped raw.

The easygoing facade he'd worn for Kayla was gone. All that remained right then was animal instinct. He hadn't realized just how wild he'd be after claiming Kayla.

A little matter of betrayal could break a guy.

But he didn't want Billy sniffing around her. Pity he needed the shifter, for the moment. A moment that wouldn't last much longer if Billy kept pushing and eyeing Kayla like she was some kind of tasty meal.

Kayla's feet crunched over the gravel driveway. Gage turned and took in her wide eyes as she gazed down at Billy.

What? Like this was the first time she'd seen a guy get decked? In her line of work, not likely.

"She doesn't look like much of a hunter," Davis noted, and he was still rubbing his chin. Davis always did that. An old habit. His eyes swept over her. "Kinda small, don't you think? A little weak."

That whipped her gaze off Billy and got it locked on the other wolf.

"Looks can be deceiving," Gage replied. Who knew that fact better than shifters?

Most folks—those who knew the truth about supernaturals, anyway—thought that shifters were born to deceive. A beast, wearing the skin of a man or woman. How did you get more deceptive than that?

Shifters were good at lying. Tricking. And killing.

Kayla's head turned toward him. Her eyes weren't flashing her emotions. No, she had whatever emotions she was feeling masked too tightly.

Humans were good at deceit, too.

She kept walking until she was by his side. "You didn't make any calls once we left the hotel."

There hadn't been a need. Gage shrugged and knew the gesture would say, *yeah, so?*

He saw the understanding in her eyes and the flush of fury on her cheeks. *Her mask was fading.*

"You really did know what I was," Kayla snapped. "The whole time, you knew."

Ah, but knowing was just the first part. Knowing and actually springing his trap—two whole different things.

But Gage let a cold smile lift his lips. He had to do the show right. "Hunters have been after my pack ever since the moment we took over this town." And that's what he'd done —taken over. Every paranormal in the city knew that Gage's pack were the ones in power. They'd kicked demon butt, terrorized the vamps, and made sure that the fools knew who was dominating Sin City. It had been perfect.

Then the hunters had come along and started their dumbass little cat and mouse game. Supernaturals had been dying. Going missing.

He'd lost two wolves.

No more.

When members of his pack had fallen under the gun, Gage had known it was time to attack. He just hadn't realized part of his attack plan would be so sweet. At least, not until he'd met Kayla.

Now she was bound to him, body and soul, just as he was bound to her. A shifter and a hunter. How insane.

He caught her hand and led her toward the cabin. For the first time, the lady dug in her heels, and his jaw almost dropped. *Now?* Now she was gonna start fighting?

Not when they'd jumped from the window.

Not when they'd been in the hotel parking lot and she could have escaped.

Not even when they'd been at that shady gas station.

Now?

The timing was so perfect, he almost smiled.

Instead, he tightened his hold on her and hauled her closer. "You need me to carry you in?" Gage injected a note of menace in the words. He was rather proud of that low growl.

Her breath huffed out. "Maybe you're forgetting, I *dropped* that knife, I—"

He heaved her over his shoulder. Kayla was in one serious fighting mood now and she kicked and punched and, *ouch*, hell, yeah, he'd have bruises from that one.

Luckily, he healed fast.

She didn't though, so he made sure his hold didn't hurt her. Unbreakable, yes, but painful? Not to her. Hurting her wasn't part of the plan he'd crafted. But he knew some pain couldn't be avoided, no matter how hard he tried.

As they headed for the cabin, Billy rose from the ground and swiped away the blood that dripped from his nose.

Gage spared him one glance. "We gonna have a problem?" If they were, he was more than ready to kick ass. This, too, was part of the plan.

Kayla dug her nails into his back, and he almost shuddered. Did she know he liked that?

Later.

Billy shook his head. "No."

"Good," Gage all but purred the words. "Now go stand guard." *Because company will be coming.* Soon.

Davis dogged Gage's steps as he made for the cabin. Kayla was yelling now, at the top of her very powerful lungs. Yells wouldn't do her any good. The ones close enough to hear her weren't exactly the helping sort.

"You sure this is a good idea?" Davis's voice was low. "Maybe you should just kill her and dump her—"

Gage knew his lethal gaze had stopped the tumble of his enforcer's words. Davis had always been too quick to kill. Gage had recognized that weakness, but he'd still taken the shifter into the pack. He'd needed Davis's strength, and he'd thought that the pack bond might temper the beast's savagery.

Maybe I thought wrong.

Kayla stopped struggling. Even over her own screams, she would have heard Davis's dark words. Figured.

"I'm not done with her yet," Gage said, and that was all that he'd say to the enforcer. "Now guard the fucking perimeter and make sure we don't have any uninvited guests."

A muscle jerked in Davis's jaw, but he didn't argue. Good. Gage took Kayla up the cabin steps and inside. He kicked the door closed and dropped her on the floor. Not too hard, but, she *had* pulled a knife on him.

Drop. Her sweet ass slammed into the old, hard wood.

"This makes two times, *wife*," he said deliberately as he leaned his shoulders back against the doorframe, "that I've carried you over the threshold."

She shoved the hair out of her eyes. Oh, yes, those golden eyes blazed with fury. "I'm not a sack of fucking potatoes!"

No, she wasn't. He didn't want to fuck potatoes.

Kayla leapt to her feet. "I *protected* you! Dumbass wolf! I. Protected. You!"

The anger in his own gut burned. Gage lunged forward and made sure he towered over her. "You set me up."

"I—" Kayla snapped her lips closed then gave a curt nod. "Fine, I did."

He blinked at the easy admission. He hadn't quite been expecting things to move so fast.

"But..." Her chin tipped up. Every time she did that, he wanted to kiss her right on that stubborn, sexy chin. "But I didn't go for your heart when I had the chance."

Didn't she? Why the hell did she think they were in this mess? "I saw the knife. Most wives don't exactly go around bringing silver knives into bed with them."

Her arms crossed over her chest. Did she huff? Sounded like it, and then she said, "I'm not most wives."

No, she wasn't. Gage stepped away from her and paced around the room. The place was pretty bare as far as furniture was concerned. An old, sagging bed. A wooden table. Two chairs. A dark brown refrigerator that hummed.

The cabin wasn't a place of comforts. He used this area for only one reason—interrogation.

It was the perfect place to learn the truth from his enemies. And the desert was perfect for making unwanted bodies disappear.

He'd buried his share of enemies out there. Vegas could be vicious. Only the strong survived. The weak? They fed the animals in the desert.

He circled around her and headed toward the fridge. Gage grabbed a small bottle of water and drained it in just a few gulps.

The wooden floor creaked beneath Kayla's feet. "So you really knew who I was, the whole time?"

He sat the bottle aside and turned back to her. "Yeah, I did."

Her chin was still up, but he saw the move for the defense that it was more than anything else. "Then why marry me?" Kayla asked.

Wasn't that the big, old million dollar freaking question? "I didn't do it because my *boss* told me to." The jab burst from him. He didn't have a boss. Others jumped when he crooked his finger.

Kayla flinched. "That wasn't why I married you."

Did he look stupid? Was he supposed to buy her BS because she was good in bed? *Very good.* "How many?" Gage gritted out, and his claws were ripping from his fingertips. Faint lines of red bled into his vision. The wolf inside wanted *out.*

"How many what?" Kayla fired right back as her brows rose, and her small fists went to her hips.

"How many men have you screwed for the sake of your

cause?" He'd like to kill them all. Every single one. Slowly. Painfully. The wolf was good at giving pain. "In order to get close, how many times did you strip and—"

She moved fast for a human. No wonder she was such a good hunter. In two seconds, she was across the room. Her index finger jabbed into his chest. "Watch it, wolf, or you'll make me lose my temper."

Right. Because that was scary. Last week, he'd beheaded a four-hundred-year-old Born vampire. So compared to him, a curvy brunette was oh-so-terrifying.

He lifted his claws and let them skate down her cheek. "Don't make me lose mine." His threat was lethal. Or it should have been, but it was complete bullshit. He'd never use his claws on her. He'd already seen the marks on her beautiful skin. When they'd made love, he'd felt her scars.

Other wolves had sliced her sweet flesh. He never would.

Her breath stilled on a rasp, but she met his gaze. No fear showed on her face. She should have been terrified. Instead, her lips tightened, and she bit out, "None, okay? There haven't been any others."

Wait...*none?*

"Despite what you think..." She jabbed him again with that finger. "I'm not a whore. I don't sleep with men just because of my job." Then she whirled away.

I hurt her. Her shoulders were up, her back straight, and Gage felt like shit. But he still asked, "So what made me different?" As a hunter, she should have been repulsed by him. All the other hunters he'd met sure had been.

Hunters. Humans who'd learned the paranormal score and were out to keep the world safe—by getting rid of all the supernaturals.

They were as vicious as any shifter, as ruthless as the

vamps, and as conniving as the demons. In short, hunters could be damn near perfect at killing. Unless you found their weak spot.

His gaze drifted over Kayla's body. *Hello, weak spot.*

"Maybe I wanted you," she said, not glancing back at him, but striding slowly toward the opposite wall.

Good thing she wasn't looking or she would have seen his shock.

"Sometimes, you want something so badly that you'll do *anything* to get what you want." Her voice had dropped, but because of his enhanced hearing, he had no trouble making out her words

You'll do anything to get what you want. He knew that feeling. Hell, he was *looking* at the thing he wanted most.

Enough to risk the pack.

She turned to face him and her features were a blank mask once again. "So, no," she said, "I didn't *screw* you for the job. I did that part all for myself. Because I wanted to be with you." Kayla shook her head. "Sometimes, I make dumb choices. Sue me."

He'd rather screw her again. And again. But they'd get to that fun task soon enough.

"What's your excuse?" Kayla wanted to know as one dark eyebrow rose. "So you tagged me as a hunter day one, fine, I get that. Go you. But why keep pretending? Why do the whole courting bit? Why marry me?"

Was she really that blind? Had to be. Otherwise she'd realize she was the one who held all the real power. "Poor little hunter." He shook his head and tried to look like he felt sorry for her. "What happened to make you this way?"

Her other eyebrow arched, and a faint line appeared between her brows.

"So untrusting," Gage continued slowly, softly, and the

memory of her scars beneath his mouth flashed through him. *Poor little hunter.*

"You're a *werewolf*, of course, I don't trust you!"

"Wolf shifter," Gage corrected as he cleared his throat. She knew the distinction. Calling him a werewolf was just insulting. "The moon doesn't make me howl. I do that, whenever I want." Nothing controlled him. No one. Werewolves were monsters made up by Hollywood. He was the real deal.

"And you do whatever you want, right?" she snapped. Her hands were fisted. Someone was feeling all feisty. Good. He didn't like her emotionless mask.

"Yes," he told her clearly, "I do." That was the benefit of being alpha.

"No matter who you hurt."

Ah, now she was getting personal. "I've never physically hurt you." Wouldn't. He protected those who fell under his charge, and he'd *never* attacked an innocent. No matter what the supernatural rumor mill might say.

But other wolf shifters weren't like him. There were some psychotic bastards running around loose in the world. He knew it, and the scars on Kayla's body said she knew it, too. Of all the shifters, the wolves were the ones who danced the closest to the edge of insanity. Their beasts were just too strong to always be controlled by the men and women who carried them.

Wolf shifters needed a pack to hold them in check. To provide them with security. *That* was why he'd started the Vegas pack. Someone strong had needed to come in and take over, and the wolves—hell, yes, they'd needed to band together. No one wanted to start a bloodbath. No one wanted to turn feral.

But sometimes, no matter what you wanted, the beast

could still take over. He thought of Kayla's scars again. The lightly raised marks on the curve of her hip and on her shoulder. The narrow lines that slid down beside her spine. Someone had hurt her badly. From the looks of those scars, the wounds had occurred long ago.

When she'd just been a kid.

"In the dark, all monsters aren't the same," he said and tried to keep his voice emotionless. A hard task, when so many emotions wanted to break free. But Kayla should know this truth already. Good and evil didn't really exist. The lines were too blurred for that vague distinction in the paranormal world.

Her lashes lowered to shield her gaze. "I know. That's why you don't have a silver knife in your heart."

Bloodthirsty little vixen. He'd known she'd make the perfect alpha female. You had to be willing to fight to the end in order to be an alpha.

Kayla was a fighter.

"You were the wrong bait," he said simply. The words were the truth. "Your bastard of a boss should have been brave enough to come after me himself." Instead of hiding in the shadows and slowly picking off the paranormals who crossed his path.

Instead of taking my wolves. Two wolves gone. He had better get them back.

Now that he had Kayla with him, it was gonna be his turn to use her as bait. He sighed, and with a genuine trace of regret, told her, "I'm sorry."

Her lashes lifted, and she frowned at him. "For what? Kidnapping me? Bringing me to this rundown shack?"

Hardly. Those were just the start of his sins. Gage waved them away with a negligent flick of his fingers. "For what's coming." Then he took her chin in his hand but kept his touch featherlight. He could already hear the approach of vehicles outside. The others had come much faster than he'd anticipated.

Gage had thought that he'd have at least another hour. But, no, the guests had arrived too soon.

They shouldn't have gotten to the scene so quickly, not unless—*dammit.*

His hands swept down Kayla's body. *Idiot.* He should have realized the truth sooner. She'd come far too willingly. He'd thought she was just changing her mind about him. That she wanted to escape with him.

But she'd still been setting him up.

His hand slid under her shirt.

She slapped at him. "*Now* isn't the time for this!"

"You've got a tracker on you." Shit. Shit, *shit.* And all those scars that pissed him off—one of them could easily have been left on her body when a tracking device was implanted. Hunters often used those devices, he knew that. But he'd been thinking with his dick, not his head. *Should have checked her.* He should have sliced beneath her skin and checked like he would have with any other hunter.

Only she wasn't any other hunter. She was...Kayla. *Mine.*

As he patted her down, her eyes widened, then she gave a slow, negative shake of her head. "Stop the frisking routine, okay? I don't have a tracker." Her words rushed out quickly.

But would she even know if she'd been tagged? Or would her boss want to keep secret watch on her and all his other hunters? "You chose the wrong side for this fight."

She swallowed. Her lips trembled a bit but she said, "I chose the only side I could."

Those approaching cars were getting closer. He could

hear the crunch of gravel beneath the tires. Either she was tagged for tracking or the dark suspicion that he'd had for weeks was true.

If Kayla didn't have a tracker on her, then he could have a traitor in the pack. Because he had *not* been followed from Vegas. He'd made sure of that fact.

"When your team comes, what will you do?" His claws were pushing through his fingertips. "Go running back to them?"

Her gaze stayed locked on his. "I'm not going back."

Well, well. Exactly what he wanted to hear, but Gage didn't let his expression alter. "Good." Then, since she deserved to know, he added, "Because I wasn't giving you up." Just so they were clear.

Her lips parted in surprise.

Time was running out. Those vehicles would be braking any minute. Before the hunters came storming in, he wanted his taste to be on her. Wanted her taste on *his* lips. So Gage stepped forward and pulled her close. His head dipped toward her, and he kissed her with the wild need that pounded through him.

What they had, it wasn't about hunter and prey. It was man and woman. Lust. Need. A desire that couldn't be satisfied, not with just one night.

Maybe not even with a thousand nights.

"We're just getting started," he promised against her lips. *His.* His wife. His for-fucking-ever. Just let the hunters try to take her. He was more than ready to rip them apart.

And they *were* coming. So big. So tough. So stupidly sure of themselves.

Pity. This time, he'd used the bait—and they were the ones running into a trap.

Another kiss. Another slow lick of his lips over hers.

Then Gage pushed her back. Away from the cabin's door and windows. "Scream for me," he said.

She didn't speak.

She liked to make things hard. That was his Kayla.

"Scream," he said again and lifted his claws. He had to transform before the hunters entered the cabin. During those few moments that it took to shift, he was vulnerable. Open for their attack. He wouldn't be vulnerable before them.

But once he was in his full wolf form...

Ready for hell, hunters?

He smiled and knew that his growing fangs would show. "Your scream will distract them when they rush inside. They'll want to help you." While he had the chance to attack them. "Time to pick your side, wife."

Then the fire of the change swept through him. A white-hot explosion of pain as his bones broke and reshaped. As his muscles stretched and his body contorted. Fur burst along his flesh. His hands became paws. His body hit the floor, and when he opened his mouth again, the growl of a beast broke from his lips.

His gaze found Kayla's. She stood where he'd left her, against the wall. Her eyes were on his. Wide. Deep. Afraid?

Another growl came from him as he took a step toward her. He could smell her fear. A hunter, afraid of the prey she'd deliberately sought out. What the hell?

She could handle him as a man, but his beast made her shake. A normal reaction for most humans, but Kayla was far from normal. He'd find out the rest of her secrets. He had to.

But right then he leapt for the shadows on the other side of the room. The hunters were closing in now. Three, two—

The cabin's door burst open. The men rushed inside.

Still wearing their dark clothes and with ski masks over their heads. The muzzles of their guns swept the room—and froze on Kayla.

Bait.

"I told you she didn't go willingly," one of the men said. The leader. The leader always talked first and stormed onto the scene like he was some big deal. Gage had learned that lesson long ago. He watched, still and silent, as the jerk in charge pushed past the others and hurried to Kayla's side. "Where the hell is he?" A demand as he reached for Kayla's arm. "Where—"

Gage's snarl seemed to echo in the small cabin.

Three men. One wolf. Perfect odds.

Gage leapt forward. Clawed the weapon from the first fool's hand. Used his teeth on the second. They screamed and yelled, and their blood flowed.

Too easy.

The wounded men tried to slip back out the door. Fleeing. He guessed the humans couldn't handle a little pain. Hunters weren't big on courage.

Except for Kayla.

His head swung back toward her. That jerk with her was aiming his gun. The muzzle pointed right at Gage. Was that supposed to scare him? His hind legs shoved down, and he leapt into the air. Gage wasn't faster than a bullet, so he'd take the hit, but then he'd take out the fool who—

"*No!*" Kayla shoved the hunter's weapon away.

Choose your side. It looked like she just had.

"Kayla, what the hell—" The human began, but that was all he had the chance to say. Gage's paws drove onto his chest as he took the hunter down. They hit the floor, and the human tried to jerk away.

Gage wasn't letting him go. The leader was the one he

wanted. The one that he'd use to break the group targeting his pack. Gage brought his mouth to the hunter's throat. He could rip the man wide open in less time than it took to breathe.

"Don't!" But, suddenly, Kayla was there. Coming right up next to the beast. "Don't hurt him. Please." A ragged breath slipped from her. "He's my brother."

Gage felt an ice-cold pain in his chest. So cold. But since when did the cold burn?

As the cold spread through him, the wolf slumped away from the hunter on the ground, and he knew he'd made a fatal mistake. He'd been distracted. He'd heard Kayla's cry, and his attention had slipped away from the hunter for a dangerous moment.

Second weapon. He should have known the prick would have one. All damn hunters did.

The asshole in the ski mask still had his gun up. When he'd fired, the weapon hadn't made a sound, but its bullet had torn straight into Gage's chest.

Kayla's presence should have distracted her team.

Not me.

Gage's form convulsed, and he shuddered as pain lanced through him. The pain—that was coming from the shift. His body was transforming rapidly—too rapidly—back into the body of a man. Gage stared down at his chest. That wasn't a normal bullet.

Something was hanging out of the back of that bullet. Like a—feather?

Then he knew. *Fuck me.*

He'd been hit by a tranq.

"Bastard," Gage managed to wheeze the word. Speech was near damn impossible. He couldn't control his body.

Couldn't stop the shift. Couldn't do anything but hit the floor as the tranquilizer poured through his veins.

"What have you done?" Kayla's voice came from a distance. She sounded afraid. Angry. Then she was crouching over him. Touching him. Holding him. "Gage?"

He couldn't speak.

The hunter could. "So it's true. The others told me, they said you were getting too close to him." Disgust flowed through the man's words.

Why couldn't he feel Kayla's fingers against his skin?

"I didn't want to believe it." The floor creaked as the hunter came closer to her. "Not *you*. You couldn't be working with a dirty animal like him."

Things were starting to dim. Just how much of a dose had the SOB emptied into him?

"Help us, Jonah," Kayla said. She was pleading with the man. "Help me get him out of here before the others—"

Too late.

More footsteps raced from outside. More humans coming in, when the wolves should have been there to have his back. Understanding hit him even as he fought to hold on to consciousness. Kayla had been telling him the truth.

No tracker. Even through the daze, he realized the significance of what was happening. Kayla hadn't led anyone to them but—

Betrayed.

The wolves who should have been there to protect him...one or both of those assholes had turned on him. His top two enforcers. His betrayers?

"I can't help you," Jonah said. "I'm sorry."

There was a whoosh of sound. A gasp. Gage managed to turn his head—it took his last bit of strength but he turned his head—and he saw the feather sticking from Kayla's chest.

The tranq worked faster on her. She fell immediately, slumping back on the floor.

The hunter's feet padded closer. The guy bent down. Put his fingers to Kayla's throat.

He still had on his ski mask, but Gage didn't need to see the man's face. He had the bastard's scent, and he'd be able to track him any place. Brother or not, Gage told him, "Y-you're...dead."

Through the eyeholes in the ski mask, the one she'd called Jonah stared back at him with a golden gaze that was an exact shade to match Kayla's. "No, wolf, you are."

The darkness swept over Gage, but he still smiled as the drugs pumped through him. Smiled because he knew the hunter was wrong. And when Gage woke again, he'd make sure the hunter got just what he deserved.

Chapter Four

She was in a cage.

Kayla's head hurt, pounded like a freaking bitch, and she was *caged*.

The cage was the first thing she noticed when she opened her eyes. Rather hard to miss it since the bars were over her head where a ceiling should be.

Holding prison. Yeah, dammit, she knew this place. She'd seen a unit like this plenty of times before. A cage to hold shifters.

I'm not a shifter.

"Hello, sweetheart."

She was just married to one.

Her head turned slowly to the left as she followed the sound of that deep voice, and that was when she noticed the second big important fact of the moment. She wasn't alone in that cage. A big, half-naked, *pissed* Gage was beside her. Jeans hung low on his hips. Just jeans, no other clothing. Not even shoes. And...and he was chained to her.

A silver handcuff circled his right wrist. A chain extended from that cuff—extended about five feet—then ended in the matching silver cuff that locked around her left wrist.

"What the hell?" She jumped off the small bed. More of a cot than anything else. The bars of their cage were silver, she knew that. The better to keep the wolves in place. Because every time they touched silver, they could burn.

She grabbed Gage's wrist. The skin was an angry red. Blistered.

"Don't worry," he told her, with a flash of his crooked half-smile, "you can kiss it later and make it all better."

She dropped his hand.

He grabbed hers right back as the smile vanished from his face. "I'm killing him."

The cold knot in her stomach told her exactly who he was taking about. "Don't." How had things gotten so screwed to hell and back? "He's all I have left."

"Then he shouldn't have fucking *shot* you."

She had nothing to say to that snarl. The chain hung between them. With her free hand, she reached up and rubbed her chest. It hurt, ached, and she knew there'd be one shiner of a bruise on her where she'd taken the tranq.

How could she explain this? Right then, she was more than ready to tear off Jonah's head, but he really was all that she had left. "He's had a hard time with wolves."

"Yeah, cry me a bleeding river." Gage's eyes blazed at her. "The dick shot his own sister, so I don't care what kind of sob story you spin. He's a dead man."

She glanced over her shoulder because she didn't want to look in his eyes anymore. She wasn't going to let him go after her brother, but she wasn't about to argue right then, not with cameras on them.

And she was sure they were being watched. Her gaze went to the left. The right. Ah, yes, there. Nestled in the far corner of the room. The slowly rotating camera had to be recording their every move.

Rats in a cage. No, wolves in a cage.

But just why were they still alive? Her, okay, sure, she was human, so they wouldn't just bury a silver bullet in her heart and dump her body. But Gage? He was at the top of Lyle's most wanted list.

So why was he caged and not killed?

"Is this the MO?" Gage wanted to know, and he tugged on her wrist to pull her attention back to him. "You catch the wolves, then you lock them up here?"

She licked her lips. "Sometimes."

"And sometimes you just kill them."

Her gaze snapped back to his. "The only shifters we hunt are those who've been preying on humans. *Killing* humans. What are we supposed to do? Let human cops go after them?" Her laugh was bitter. She'd learned the brutal truth about the way that worked when she'd been sixteen. "Human cops wouldn't be able to handle the monsters." That was why her team was called in.

"But you can," he said flatly.

"I can." Whispered. Her team could. Lyle's group was contracted by Uncle Sam. The government knew all about supernaturals, and they paid a good penny to make sure that the right people—the right hunters—went after their vicious prey.

They weren't just randomly picking up supernaturals. Not all the supernaturals out there were even dangerous. But some *were* real-life nightmares that couldn't be stopped by normal means. Lyle's team hunted the cases that no one else could manage.

They stopped the killers. Took out the nightmares.

Gage's brows lifted as he glanced around the cage. "You're doing a real top job of handling things now."

"Screw you, wolf." She spun away. Paced as far as the chain would let her. Kayla was in this whole messed up situation because she'd lusted after the wolf. She should've known better. Actually, she *had* known better.

"I don't prey on humans," Gage said, his voice quiet. "I never have."

Her fingers wrapped around the bars. The cage was built to keep supernaturals in. Would a human be able to find a way out? "Tell that to Slater Hawk." Hawk's case had been the one to pull her in on the hunt for Gage Riley. Slater Hawk had been sliced apart and then dumped in the desert.

"Since he's burning with the devil, I won't tell Hawk anything." How could a man's voice sound so careless when he was talking about death? "But believe me, that torturing SOB got exactly what he deserved."

Her heart raced faster. This was what she'd suspected. The reason she hadn't driven her knife into Gage's chest. "Why? Why'd you kill him?"

"Because he was a twisted bastard who carved up four showgirls in the city. I don't like it when women get hurt."

She'd heard about the attacks on those ladies, only Lyle had told her that the wolves had been behind them. And he'd had proof, not just some BS story. She glanced back at Gage. "Why kill a human when your own pack was really slaughtering those women?" Had Hawk just found out the truth? "I saw the pictures," she told him. The poor women. Brutalized. Tortured. "I know the difference between claw marks and stab wounds." This wasn't amateur hour. She knew the difference, far better than most.

She'd carry claw marks on her body until the day she died.

The chain clinked against the floor as Gage moved toward her. "If you cut off a shifter's hand while he's in animal form, that limb never shifts back. Certain hunters take shifter body parts like that as trophies." His hands closed over her shoulders, and he leaned in close to her. "But you knew that, sweetheart." His breath feathered over her ear. "Didn't you?"

Her eyes closed. He was too close to her. And she was too weak where he was concerned. "You-you're saying that Hawk killed a shifter and used—"

"*No.*" Snapped out. "I'm saying someone gave Hawk that claw, someone set the pit bull out, and got him to carve up those women so that my pack would look guilty."

Her eyes opened as she spun to fully face. Dread was a cold knot in her stomach. "Why?"

Metal screeched behind her. She didn't look back. She knew that sound. The heavy metal entrance door was being shoved across the stone floor, screeching and groaning like an old man in pain.

Gage smiled at her, and the sight was grim. "Ask your boss."

Slowly, Kayla peered back over her shoulder. Sure enough, her boss, Lyle McKennis, stalked toward them. As usual, he was perfectly styled. His dark hair was slicked back. His suit was wrinkle free. And his handsome face even sported a wide grin.

Her heart beat faster. Whenever Lyle smiled like that, it was a bad sign.

Very, *very* bad.

The door slammed closed behind him.

* * *

Jonah stared down at the computer monitor. On that monitor, he could clearly see that the wolf was touching Kayla again. That jerk was *always* touching her, and she didn't seem to mind at all.

What the hell was wrong with her? After all they'd been through together. *Why?* Why would she side with a beast now?

She had to hate the shifters as much as he did. They were all monsters. They destroyed everyone and everything they touched.

And she'd married one of those freaks?

He'd thought it was just cover. Just her following orders. Until he'd seen the way she touched the guy back at that cabin. When the wolf had fallen, she'd rushed to his side. Her fingers had trembled. There'd been fear in her voice.

Then when she'd looked at Jonah, he'd seen the anger in her eyes. His big sis had been furious at him for taking down her wolf.

"Great job," one of the other hunters praised as he slapped Jonah on his back. "Another pelt for you."

Jonah didn't respond. Did the hunter even realize that Jonah's sister was in that cage on the screen? Lyle was walking toward her now. The boss had better get her out of there. Sure, Kayla had made the wrong choice, but Jonah wasn't gonna let her be caged.

I shouldn't have shot her.

His stomach twisted and bile rose in his throat as he remembered that desperate moment. The others on his team had all been convinced that Kayla had turned traitor. He hadn't believed it, not until he'd seen the truth with his own eyes.

Bring her in or take her out.

Those had been his orders, and he sure hadn't planned to let the trigger-happy hunters with him get a shot at her. Max and Bryan tended to shoot first and celebrate immediately. Of course, right then, they weren't celebrating anything.

They were being stitched back together, courtesy of Kayla's wolf and his killer claws.

"Sorry about your sister," the hunter next to him said. Travis. One of the new guys that Lyle had brought in recently. So he *did* realize that Kayla was the one being held like an animal.

Only she's not.

"The boss will clear this up," Jonah said. Lyle had to fix this mess. Kayla was the one thing that mattered to Jonah, and he wouldn't watch as—

Lyle wasn't heading toward the cage. He walked right up to the video camera. Smiled into the lens. Then Jonah heard the boss say, "I got this," right before the lead hunter reached up and yanked out the video and audio surveillance system.

The screen before Jonah immediately went blank. What the hell? This wasn't protocol. All interrogations were to be monitored. Those were orders that came straight down from the federal government. *All* of them had to be recorded.

Jonah spun on his heel, but Travis grabbed him and pulled him back. "Sorry, man," Travis said, with a shake of his blond head. "But I've got orders—and you're not leaving this room."

The door opened. Two more hunters entered the surveillance area.

"When family's involved, hell, it's just a bitch." Travis

exhaled as he shook his head again. "You just sit tight, and this will all be over soon."

The hell it would.

* * *

"WHAT ARE YOU DOING, LYLE?" Kayla demanded, grabbing at the bars with white-knuckled fists. "That camera is always supposed to stay on!"

Gage realized that his little hunter sounded furious.

She didn't realize what was happening.

Gage stood in the middle of the cage—*he hated cages*—and watched silently as the one she'd called Lyle turned to face them. What the bastard was doing was pretty obvious.

He was making sure he didn't have an audience for this little party. And Gage knew exactly *why*.

Laughter pulled from him. Deep. Mocking. Did the hunters even realize what was happening?

Lyle smiled, flashing white and very sharp teeth.

"You know, for a hunter," Gage kept his voice bland, "you sure as shit smell like a shifter." Because there was no mistaking that scent. Wild. Woodsy. *Animal.*

It was a little bonus that Mother Nature had given the supernaturals. They could always recognize their own kind. Demons could always see right through the glamour and find their brethren. Witches could feel the pull of magic exerted by others like them.

As for shifters? One smell was all it took to recognize another animal.

Kayla's shoulders stiffened. She was still staring at Lyle, but the tension in her body was suddenly screaming.

Only she *wasn't* screaming. When she spoke, her words

were soft. "You're wrong. Lyle McKennis is the lead hunter in the area. He can't be a shifter."

"Why?" Gage asked as Lyle kept the smile on his face. "Because he's the big, bad boss who's sent you out to kill the shifters in this town? Sorry, sweetheart, but our kind has a long and vicious history of turning on each other."

Only Lyle had gotten smart. The jerk didn't have a pack of his own, so he'd tricked humans into killing for him.

Shifters truly were very good at lying.

Lyle was almost at the cage now.

"That's not true," Kayla retorted and gave a fast, negative shake of her head. "He's the one who found me and Jonah after—after our parents were killed. He saved us, got us help—"

Fast as a striking snake, Lyle's hand shot through the cage bars. His claws were out, and they shoved right against Kayla's throat. "And I'm the one who's gonna kill you, too, if you don't do exactly what I say."

He was a dead man.

Gage rolled his shoulders. He let his own claws break from his fingertips. "I'm guessing you don't want to die easily," he noted in a considering way as he studied the other shifter. "You want me to take my time with things. Strip away your flesh. Make you beg and scream before I give you that fucking sweet release of death." The guy had to want that or else he wouldn't be touching Kayla.

Lyle's green eyes narrowed. He was staring at Kayla, not Gage. And the bastard *needed* to move those damn claws away from her.

Gage's nostrils flared. A new scent had hit the air. Blood. Kayla's blood.

A snarl sprang from his lips, and he leapt those few feet that would take him to the side of the cage. He slashed out with his own claws, and if Lyle had moved even one second slower, he would have cut the bastard's hand off.

"Don't fucking touch her. " Gage's lethal order was the growl of a beast. His wolf wanted out. Sure, wolves liked the scent of blood just as much as any shifter, but not when that scent belonged to a mate.

And Kayla was most definitely *his*.

When the blood scent came from a mate, the wolf within just wanted to destroy any threat near her.

Lyle had backed up and made sure to get clear of the cage. His cocky smile was back. "I thought it might be like that. I mean, I knew the truth about her for years. I figured if I just put her in the right wolf's path..."

Gage pulled Kayla away from the bars. He looked at her throat and lightly touched the tender skin. Just scratches, but he understood the point Lyle had wanted to make.

I can kill her. You can watch.

Screw that.

This Lyle asshole could watch while Gage cut *him* open.

"What truth?" Kayla demanded as she batted Gage's hands away.

It was Lyle's turn to laugh now. "Why, exactly, do you think your wolf married you? Because he took one look at you and fell in love?" His voice mocked her.

How could they get out of the cage? How could he shut that jerk's mouth?

Kayla's breath heaved. "I don't understand. What is happening?"

"You're a potential mate for a wolf shifter. Your scent is different, at least it always was to me." Lyle's gaze darted to Gage. "And I'm betting it is to him, too. One scent, just one deep breath, and I could tell you were...ripe."

"Bastard!" Kayla screamed. "I don't—"

"Of course, you were only sixteen when we met, so I decided to give you some growing time. I knew you'd be the perfect lure that I needed." Lyle shrugged. "It's so hard to find potential mates for wolves these days. So hard, but in that bloodbath, I found *you*."

Gage barely managed to hold his wolf back. The beast was clawing him from the inside. Ripping and tearing with his fury to break loose. "What do you want?" Because the jerk had to want something. Otherwise, Gage wouldn't have woken in the cage.

He wouldn't have woken at all.

"I want your pack, and you're gonna give them to me."

"Keep wishing, asshole." He'd never turn on his pack. Pack was sacred. Pack was life.

Lyle's green eyes narrowed. "This city's mine now. I'm taking over."

It would feel so good to smash the prick's face. He could already imagine the bones crushing beneath his fist. "Is that why you sent that human to carve up the showgirls? Because you were taking over?" And using Hawk to do his dirty work for him.

Some humans didn't mind getting their hands bloody. Some liked the blood. Some, like Hawk.

Lyle just smiled as his canines lengthened. "I've always found humans to be very accommodating."

"I'm gonna kill you." The snarled threat wasn't Gage's this time—it was Kayla's. Now she'd broken through her shock and was going right for the rage stage of the game. Good for her.

They'd need her rage.

"Doubtful." Lyle didn't look worried at all. The guy just shrugged again and rocked back on his heels. "You've always rather lacked what I think of as the killer instinct. Some humans have it."

Hawk came to mind. That bastard had refused to turn on Lyle all the way to the end. No matter how much pain Gage had given to him. *I gave him plenty. Payback for pain he gave those women.*

"Some don't," Lyle finished. His gaze hardened on Kayla. "But if you don't do exactly as I say, I promise, I'll bring your brother to you in pieces."

Kayla sucked in a sharp breath. Hell. The brother was gonna be a problem for them. Gage hadn't counted on that attachment when he'd been doing all his grand planning.

Lyle obviously had.

When Lyle's gaze turned back to him, Gage knew the other shifter had planned for all sorts of fucking situations. "Your pack," Lyle said, almost snarling. "I know you got them to pull from the city. To *hide.* That's not gonna work. They aren't gonna stay in the shadows and then jump out and try to take me down."

Actually, they were. That was *his* plan.

"So you'll take me to them," Lyle crossed his arms over his chest, stretching his fancy suit. "And I'll take them out."

So there'd be only one top dog in Sin City.

"Not happening." Gage hadn't built that pack from the ground up just to watch the wolves get destroyed.

Lyle pointed to Kayla. "Then she'll be the one in pieces." He turned away. Strolled toward the door like he didn't have a care in the world. "You've got an hour. So I'd suggest you start rethinking that position of yours." He reached for the heavy door handle, then glanced back. "Because it's so hard to find a good mate these days."

Then he was gone. The metal clang of the shutting door

echoed through the room, and Gage swore in disgust and fury.

That sonofabitch wasn't going to push him into a corner. Lyle wasn't destroying the pack that Gage had built, and Lyle damn well wasn't hurting Kayla.

Not while I'm still breathing.

Kayla glanced over at him. For a tough hunter, she sure looked vulnerable. No, *broken.*

Especially with the faint drops of blood on her neck.

"He was...he was the only person who kept me going after my parents died." Her voice was softer, huskier, than he'd ever heard before. "Lyle found me, alone in that house with their bodies. I was holding Jonah. Trying to stop the bleeding and *save* him—"

Gage didn't speak when she broke off and inhaled on a deep, shuddering breath. He just waited. She needed to put these pieces together faster. Didn't she realize yet what had happened? As soon as he'd seen Lyle—as soon as he'd caught the bastard's scent, Gage had known the truth.

"Lyle said he was a hunter." Her shoulders hunched even as she wrapped her arms around her stomach, as if she were trying to hug herself. Or to guard herself. "Th-that he'd tracked the wolf shifter. That he was there to help us."

Only Gage bet that if Kayla hadn't been so wild with her grief at the time, she would have seen the blood on the man's fingers. Wild with grief and too young.

You were only sixteen when we met, so I decided to give you some growing up time. The bastard's words rang through his mind. "You were just a kid. You didn't realize what he was."

She hadn't realized that her savior was the monster who'd been at the door. The monster who'd destroyed her life.

Her hands fell to her sides as she lifted her chin. The gesture almost broke his heart. "He...killed them? My parents?" Her fingers rose to rub against her shoulder. He knew a line of scars was beneath her shirt. Right in that exact spot. He'd kissed those scars during that too short night at the hotel. "Lyle was the wolf who tried to kill me?" she asked, but he knew the words weren't a question, not really.

Kayla had realized the truth. After all Lyle had said, she had to know it now.

Dammit, he hated this. She shouldn't look broken. Broken wasn't his Kayla. Strong. Fierce. *That* was her. Not this lost shell. She looked like she'd just lost everything. She hadn't. Didn't she see that?

Gage caught her arms. Pulled her close. "When he cut you, he knew." Sometimes, wolves could recognize potential mates from a scent, just like the bastard had said. But if blood was involved, oh, yeah, that recognition level amped way the hell up.

Blood always tells.

"Knew what?" A faint line was between her brows. "That I'm some predestined wolf mate? That's bullshit!"

Now a little spark was coming back. He didn't want a spark. He wanted a raging inferno. "There's nothing predestined about it. Certain people are genetic matches for shifters. It's DNA, not a merging of the souls." Some human females could carry a hybrid shifter child. Some couldn't. Science.

But women like her were getting rarer each day. Had that been the reason Lyle first attacked her? Maybe he'd thought her mother was a match, but then he'd found an easier target just waiting there in the house for him.

"He won't kill you," Gage said with certainty. His fingers flexed against her skin. Soft. Weak. Human.

"He won't get the chance," Kayla fired right back and even though it looked like tears might be glistening in her eyes, her voice cut better than any shifter's claws. Good. "I'll take his heart first, then shove it right down that bastard's throat."

Ah, my sweet inferno. There was the woman he wanted.

"Only if you beat me to the attack," Gage told her. She wouldn't. "Now, sweetheart, it's time for us to get the hell out of here." Because while Lyle might not actually carry through on his threat to kill Kayla, the bastard would no doubt get off on hurting her.

Won't happen.

Or maybe Lyle would just kill her brother.

And she'll break apart then.

Gage couldn't let her break.

There were whispers about wolves in the paranormal circles. Of all the supernaturals out there, the wolf shifters were the most unstable. The most given to insanity. Unless they had the security and the strength of a pack, their primal natures could take over with dangerous consequences.

Wolves weren't meant to be alone.

But Lyle was alone.

And from what Gage had seen, Lyle was most definitely psychotic. The sooner he was dead, the better.

* * *

LYLE WALKED SLOWLY down the hallway. He didn't glance back at the holding cell. There was no point in looking back.

There never was.

Kayla knew the truth about him now. Good. He was getting rather tired of hiding himself.

A hunter passed and nodded his head toward Lyle. Lyle's back teeth clenched. They were all getting on his nerves.

Years...*years* he'd spent playing attack dog for Uncle Sam. Being the federal government's bitch. At first, he'd hunted alone. So much darkness. So much blood.

"Sir." Another hunter slid by him. This one even gave him some dumbass salute. A new recruit sent up from some boot camp in the South. Did this look like the fucking military?

Lyle turned a corner and stalked into his office. He slammed the door, and realized his hands were shaking. The wolf inside wanted out. He'd denied the beast for too long. He needed to hunt. To kill. Not to hide in some dank hole in the ground. Not to stand back while the blood flowed.

He liked the blood too much to just stand back. Liked the kills. The screams.

Kayla's mother had screamed. So sweetly. She'd screamed and begged, and so had Kayla. The beast had loved their cries.

The beast had wanted to rip Kayla open, and he'd slashed with his claws. That night, he'd known only blind rage and bloodlust, until he'd caught the sweet scent in the air. Until the beast had realized that Kayla Kincaid wasn't just prey. She was something more.

Something far more precious.

The man had pulled back the beast. Stopped the slaughter. Of course, it had been too late by then. Her parents had been dead. Her brother barely breathing. And Kayla—she'd been terrified.

Lyle paced to his desk. Sat down heavily in the chair, then looked down at the claws that had burst from his fingertips.

A slip. He was having more and more of them lately. If he wasn't careful, the hunters would all learn the truth about him.

He clenched his hands into fists and his claws cut right through his skin.

The beast wanted out.

And the man was just tired of fighting him. Lyle knew he was different. Too savage. Too twisted. He'd always known. But he'd tried to channel that bloodlust. To use it. He'd hunted his own kind. Tracked the deadliest paranormals.

But they weren't enough.

Sometimes, innocent blood just tasted sweeter.

His teeth were lengthening. His bones starting to pop.

No, no, he couldn't shift now. He had to hold on just a bit longer. He had a job to do. A pack to destroy.

The wolves in Vegas thought they were so smart. Banding together. Growing stronger. Wolves didn't face the risk of insanity when they were in a pack.

The pack is strength. A stupid wolf mantra his parents had told him long ago, before they'd been killed by the government. The same government that had taken Lyle in and made him into the monster he was.

The pack is life. Did Gage recite that same bullshit?

Blood smeared on his jeans. He barely felt the pain in his palms. When his claws cut him, he almost liked the flow of blood.

Almost?

If he'd had a pack, maybe things would have been

different for him. Maybe he would have controlled his beast.

Maybe not.

But the wolves in Vegas weren't any more damn special than he was. If he had to face the fury of the beast alone—day in and day out—then they should have to face it, too. They should all know what it was like to feel sanity slipping away, moment by moment, until nothing remained.

Until there was only fury. Instinct. Death.

They should *all* know.

He'd make sure they knew.

Because he was gonna rip that pack apart, even if he had to sacrifice every single hunter in his compound in order to do the job. After all, what were human lives worth? Humans were weak. Meaningless.

Only the strong survived in this world.

He was the strong. He was the alpha, and he'd prove that truth to everyone.

Chapter Five

"So how the hell do we get out of this cage?" Gage demanded, as he paced the small perimeter of their prison, and since he was pacing and they were chained, she pretty much had to pace, too.

Kayla hated the chain that bound them. And hated that she had to tell him, "We don't get out."

Those words stopped him. Gage glanced back at her. The faint lines on his face seemed deeper than before. "There's always a way out."

Such an optimistic shifter. She shook her head. "Not this time. The cell was designed for the maximum containment of a shifter. Even with your strength, you won't be able to break the bars. And when you try..." Because she suspected he was already thinking about that very thing. "The silver will just burn you. It's the purest form of silver I've ever seen." Guaranteed to make a shifter scream.

"So you're just what—giving up?"

Her eyes narrowed. Who did Gage think he was talking to? Wasn't a woman entitled to a bit of a freak out when she discovered her whole life was a lie? But she was pushing forward, and she wasn't gonna fall apart again. Kayla straightened her shoulders. "I'm picking my moment," she said, "and when the right moment comes, I'll get us out of here." The moment wasn't happening then. Sure, no cameras were on them. No other hunters listening in. But this *wasn't* the moment to escape. "In an hour, Lyle will be back."

"And you want to wait for him?" He looked at her like she was crazy.

No, what she really wanted was to slam her fist into Lyle's face. But waiting was all she could do...then. "When he opens that cage door, that's when we'll get our freedom." They just had to move fast enough and be strong enough.

They wouldn't have long, but that door *would* open. Lyle—the lying, conniving bastard—would be the one to unlock the cage.

Then it would be their turn to attack.

Gage was back to pacing. "And what if they just drug us again? Instead of opening that door wide, what if they shoot us, then drag us out of here one at a time?"

He would point out that option. She shrugged and tried to appear careless. Such an act. "Then we're screwed." Because her escape plan—the only plan that she could think of—involved Lyle opening the door for her. He opened it, then she killed him.

End of story.

Lyle had always underestimated her. She'd pushed for the more dangerous missions. He'd held her back, saying she wasn't ready.

I'll show you a killer instinct, asshole.

The chain rattled. Her gaze lifted. Gage was closing in on her, and his eyes were glowing with the light of his beast.

She held her ground. Her heart raced in her chest,

drumming fast enough to almost hurt, and she wondered just how acute his shifter senses really were.

Could he smell her fear?

If we don't get out, I die.

Because she knew that when it came down to a choice between Gage's pack and her, well, there wasn't a choice at all.

Gage might think that Lyle wouldn't actually kill her, but Kayla knew better.

Did he really kill my parents? The suspicion was in her gut, knotting deep. For years, she'd been following his orders. He'd given her a home. Given her protection.

And now he wanted to carve her up.

Like he had carved up her mother and father? He'd been there that night, but not as the rescuer she'd thought. As the monster she'd feared.

Gage's fingers rose to touch her throat. She flinched, then realized that his claws weren't out. Her breath whispered from between her lips.

"I don't like that scent from you," Gage said, his voice a dark rumble of sound.

Uh, come again?

"Fear usually smells good."

So he *could* smell it.

"But coming from you, the scent just makes me want to kill." Then he leaned forward. His arms wrapped around her, and he lifted her up against him. Gage's lips pressed against her throat. "I swear, I'll kill him."

He was kissing her wounds. His mouth was gentle, but the hands holding her were hard with strength and power.

She trembled against him as his lips moved toward her ear, and that tremble—it wasn't from fear.

I should've had more time with him.

Gage hadn't married her for love, yes, she got that part. But why couldn't they have just enjoyed a few days together? Had death really needed to come calling hours after she said "I do" with him?

Would it have been so wrong to take more pleasure? Before the pain that was promised?

I'll carve her up.

Her eyes closed. Her hands curled around his shoulders. She knew what she wanted.

They had an hour.

No cameras. No audio recordings.

An hour.

She rubbed her body lightly against his. *Take more pleasure.* Because if the escape plan forming in her mind didn't work, she'd know only pain in the time to come.

No, I want pleasure.

"I don't...I don't care why you married me." Her voice came out soft and husky.

His head lifted. She couldn't read the emotion behind the strong lines and angles of his face. And she'd always thought he seemed open? What a lie.

Shifters are born to lie. Lyle's words. She just hadn't realized—*he* was the one with the best skills at deception.

"I don't care why," she repeated. She didn't even want to talk about that genetic match bull right then. She just wanted him.

Maybe he had been playing her, the way she'd intended to play him.

Catch a hunter. Spring your trap.

They were both trapped now, and they had only each other. So she simply told Gage what she felt. "Before he comes back, I want to be with you again."

His pupils expanded until only black seemed to fill his

gaze. No more bright blue. Slowly, he lowered her to the floor. Her feet touched the stone. Okay, right, she got that this wasn't exactly the honeymoon suite. The cage bars weren't sexy. The cot was narrow. The—

"Your timing is shit," he informed her as his voice roughened with arousal.

Um, yeah, true, but it wasn't like she had a rain check option that she could offer up to him.

Gage pulled in a deep breath. "Don't cry out," he told her in that hard rasp that sent shivers skating over her body. "He'll hear, and I don't want him hearing a single sound that you make for me."

Kayla licked her lips. No screaming this time. Check. She could do that.

Could he? Gage had been pretty loud last time.

Then his hands were on her jeans. Yanking at the snap and jerking down the zipper. She kicked out of her boots and—

His fingers slid between her legs. Pushed up into her sex, and she gasped at the sensual touch. Kayla rose onto her toes, trying to adjust to the feel of those long, hard fingers inside of her. She wasn't ready, not yet, but—

His thumb pushed over her clit. His fingers withdrew. Thrust again.

Her knees did a little jiggle even as her sex tightened around his thrusting fingers. Just that fast, Kayla knew she was getting wet for him. Adrenaline and need fired her blood, and her nails scratched over his arms as she pulled him closer.

When they kissed, there was nothing soft or gentle about it. Wild. Heat. Hunger.

Craving.

If this was her last time with him, she'd take everything

he had. There was no control. No holding part of herself back. Only lust. Only him.

He ditched the jeans he'd been wearing and lifted her up into his arms. She loved his strength...when she'd feared that same strength in others. Her legs wrapped around his hips, and she held on to him as tightly as she could.

He positioned his cock at the entrance of her body. The broad head brushed against her. Teased. Only the tip slid inside. He wasn't thrusting fully yet. Gage still had his control.

She wanted that control to break. No, to shatter into a million pieces. She wanted him wild and desperate for her. The way she was for him.

Kayla's mouth broke from his. Wolves liked to bite, almost as much as vampires did. They liked their sex rough. Hard. Consuming.

Just the way she did.

Kayla pressed her mouth to his neck. Licked his skin. Gage shuddered. Good, but she wanted more. She opened her mouth. Put her teeth against him, right where the curve of his shoulder met his neck. Then she nipped him.

"Kayla."

She knew that wolves marked their mates this way. A bite to claim. Was she claiming him?

She wasn't a wolf but...

Kayla let him feel the press of her teeth once more, and she could almost hear the rip of his control.

Better.

His hands hardened on her, digging into her hips, and he thrust deep. Gage drove into her with one fierce plunge. And it was exactly what she needed. What she wanted. Each wild thrust had his cock shoving deep into her, and the sensual strokes made her whole body tighten. Pleasure. So close. So—

He took two steps, kept his tight hold on her, and Kayla found her back slammed against the cage bars. He was still thrusting into her, and she loved it. But this position, sweet hell, it made him go in even deeper.

After living the last eighteen years only feeling rage and pain, this was what she'd hoped for.

Wild and hot.

Her breath panted out. She wanted to scream as the pleasure built, but she bit her lower lip to hold back the sound. He was swelling even bigger inside of her. Going impossibly deep. *Yes.* She'd never felt more connected to another person. Never felt as if she belonged to another, the way she belonged to him.

His eyes were on hers. So intense and deep. She could see the edge of his canines. Lengthening, because the beast was close.

Then he put those canines on *her*. In nearly the exact spot that she'd bit him. Kayla arched toward him. She wasn't afraid of the beast that lurked just beneath the surface of the man. She wanted him to bite her.

But—

Gage yanked his head back. Thrust faster. One strong hand lifted and wrapped around the bar near her and she wanted to call out a warning to him. He'd be burned by the silver. It would hurt him.

Her climax hit her on a wave of pleasure so intense that every muscle in her body seemed to clench. She lost her breath, and when she opened her mouth to cry out because she couldn't hold the sound in any longer, Gage kissed her. He drove his tongue past her lips even as his cock thrust into her core.

Then he seemed to erupt within her. She could feel the jet of his release inside of her. Her sex contracted around him, greedy for the pleasure to continue. Why did it have to end? She'd just found him.

Why did everything have to be so twisted for them?

Why couldn't she just be a woman and he just be a man?

Gage's mouth slowly lifted from hers. He stared at her with the hungry, lustful eyes of a beast.

Never just a man.

He was so much more.

Her heart raced in her chest. Pounded so fast. Gage withdrew from her—dammit—and carefully lowered her to the stone floor. When her unsteady knees finally regained their strength, she remembered his hand. In the heat of the moment, Gage had actually reached out for the silver bars.

She caught his hand and winced at the angry blisters lining his palm. "Gage." His name whispered from her.

His fingers clenched into a fist. "I didn't even feel the pain."

Her gaze rose to find him watching her.

That half-smile flashed across his face. "Fucking you felt too good."

She wanted to smile back at him because that grin had always gotten beneath her skin. That grin—from the first sight, it had told her he *couldn't* be a monster, even when she knew otherwise. But Kayla couldn't smile in return. She knew what future was coming for them.

And it wasn't going to be easy or pretty or *good*. In order to escape, she'd have to turn on the men she'd worked side by side with for years.

She might even have to kill them.

Or else she and Gage would be the ones to wind up dead.

* * *

"I WANT TO SEE MY SISTER," Jonah demanded as he marched into Lyle's office. He didn't know what was going on at the compound, but he sure didn't like it. He'd been forcibly held in that surveillance room by the other hunters—*so much for friendship*—and then, twenty minutes later, when they'd finally let him go, he'd discovered that more hunters were stationed in front of Kayla's holding cell.

When he'd tried to go inside and talk to his sister, the hunters—jerks who he'd counted as friends before—had lifted their weapons toward him.

What in the hell was happening? Things couldn't have gotten this screwed, this fast. It was like a nightmare. One that he just couldn't wake up from, no matter how hard he tried.

He'd been trying pretty damn hard.

"I *want* to see her," Jonah blasted again. He had to make sure she was all right. It was his fault she was in containment. *His fault.*

Lyle leaned forward in his chair and gave a sad shake of his head. "I'm afraid that's just not possible."

"Make it possible." Lyle could do anything he wanted. The man was the head honcho at the compound. He just answered to the government guys in their fancy suits—and those guys came around only when it was prison transfer time. "Give me clearance to see her. Now." Anger had him seething. He still had his weapon. The others hadn't taken that, and if he didn't get to see his sister soon—

Lyle exhaled on a slow breath. "You know she betrayed us."

The boss's words scraped right over Jonah's soul. His jaw clenched, and he straightened to his full height. "There's been a mistake." That was what he kept telling himself. A mistake could be fixed. "If you'd just let me talk to her, I can fix things."

There was sympathy in Lyle's gaze, but he said, "She'll try to bring you over to her side, too."

"I'm not going on the side of a freaking wolf!" Not after what that shifter had done to him so long ago. *Three months.* He'd been trapped in a hospital for three months because of the beast that had come after his family. He'd nearly lost his arm. He'd been clawed open.

And his sister was siding with those monsters now?

"No." Lyle pushed to his feet and walked around his desk. "No, I never thought you'd join up with a wolf."

Jonah's breath heaved out. Right. Lyle trusted him. Lyle *knew* him.

"But then," Lyle's assessing gaze swept over him, "I never thought Kayla would, either."

Her betrayal didn't make any sense. "Why?" Why would his sister turn on the hunters, on him, for a wolf?

"Because they're fucking."

Jonah's teeth ground together so hard that it hurt. *I'll kill that wolf.* "I can—I can get her to come back to us." If he could just talk to her, he could make this all right again.

"The others know that she can't be trusted now." Lyle walked toward him with slow, measured steps. His green gaze was watchful. Always so watchful. "What we do in this world, it's life or death, and if you can't count on the hunter who's supposed to be watching your back..." He shook his head sadly. "Then just what good is that backup?"

No good. Worthless. But Kayla wasn't worthless. She was everything to him. Jonah fought to keep his voice calm. So much was happening. So much he still didn't fully understand. "Why—why'd you turn off the surveillance camera?" That hadn't been protocol. Not even close. And with Kayla there, the cameras absolutely should have been rolling.

"Because you're already in enough pain." Lyle's hand came up and clasped his shoulder. "I didn't want you to see just how far your sister has fallen. I didn't want any of the other hunters to see just how twisted she's become. They thought she was a friend, but the truth is, she's been working with Gage Riley. She's been planning—" His hand tightened on Jonah's shoulder and his words broke away.

Jonah frowned at him and knocked that comforting hand away. "Just what has she been planning?"

"She was selling us out to her wolf. Telling him where our compound was located. You want to know the real reason all of Gage Riley's pack mates vanished from the city?" The faint lines around Lyle's mouth deepened. "They're planning to attack us, and Kayla was going to help them destroy every hunter here." The briefest of pauses, then, "Every hunter, including you."

Bullshit. Kayla would never turn on him. No matter what else had happened, he wouldn't believe that. Kayla wouldn't hurt him, wouldn't turn on him—

Not the way I turned on her. He could still see her eyes. When she'd realized that he'd shot her...*betrayal.*

She was the only family he had. When he'd been in that hospital, wired to those constantly beeping machines and drugged out of his mind, Kayla had been there. Every single day. Bandaged and bruised herself, she'd held his hand.

"Everything's gonna be all right, Jonah, I promise."

Kayla's young voice. A voice that he still heard late at night, when the memory of pain and death came to him.

Jonah cleared his throat. "What's gonna happen to her?"

Lyle turned away and headed for the door. "Come now, Jonah. Do you really think I'd kill a human? *Her?*"

Yes. Because Lyle could be the coldest SOB that Jonah had ever seen.

And as his boss walked out of the room, Jonah knew... nothing would ever be *all right* again.

I'm sorry, Kayla.

* * *

"He'll be back early," Kayla said as she adjusted her clothes. Gage had already pulled back on his jeans. "No way is he going to give us an hour. Lyle will be coming back—"

"Now," Gage told her because he could hear the tread of footsteps in the hallway. Lyle had a hard step. Pushing forward with too much eagerness. The prick was hurrying down the hallway in his rush to return.

Because you want to watch us bleed.

Kayla spun back to face Gage. Her lips were still swollen from his mouth, but her face was so controlled, so determined. She was a brave one. "Once we're out of the cage, that's when we have to attack."

As long as they didn't get tranquilized or shot first, yes, that was the plan. Not a very good plan, but all they had for the moment.

She pulled on the chain. "They think this will keep us in check."

Because silver could be such a bitch to his kind.

"But you can stand the pain."

Yes, he could.

"So the silver's not a weakness. It's our advantage." She lifted the chain and met his eyes. "It's our weapon."

Hell, yes, it was. Because Lyle might not be so good at handling the pain. The bastard wasn't an alpha, no matter what he might be telling himself.

Gage smiled at her. "Anyone ever told you that you're beautiful when you're planning to kill?"

Her lips seemed to curl, just a little. "Only you."

The metal screeched as the holding room door opened.

More footsteps. Lyle came in, wearing that smug grin of his. He inhaled, then laughed, "I knew you'd just have to take that one last chance to fuck her."

And Gage had known that the SOB would catch the scent of sex on Kayla. A human wouldn't have known, but a shifter's nose? No fooling it.

Kayla's shoulders stiffened. "You've got it wrong. I'm the one who wanted the chance to fuck him."

Now Lyle's grin slipped.

Good.

But then Lyle pulled a gun from the holster on his hip. "This isn't loaded with tranqs, Kayla, my dear. And you know I'm one damn good shot. After all, I taught you, didn't I?"

The chain hung between Kayla and Gage.

"So this is what's gonna happen," Lyle said as he came closer to the cage. "I'm gonna open the cage and Kayla, you're gonna come out. I'll unchain you, and if either you or your wolf try to come at me..." He lifted the gun. Aimed it at her. "You'll get a shot right to the head. Between those pretty gold eyes of yours. Then Gage can howl over your cold, dead body."

Fury and fear swept through Gage. He'd been worried Lyle would try some shit like this.

"So you'll free me from this cage, and then do what?" Kayla demanded. No fear from her. Just anger. "Let me waltz out of this place?"

Lyle laughed. "No, of course not. I'm gonna torture you until you break." His gaze met Gage's through the bars. "Or until he does."

"I'm not the breaking type!" Kayla snapped.

"Everyone is, after a while." Lyle punched in a key code on the cage's lock, then scanned his left thumb. A soft click and whir sounded. Lyle stepped back and aimed his gun at Kayla's head once more. "Now push open the door and come on out. Then I'll uncuff you."

So the torturing fun could begin.

Kayla glanced back at Gage. "I'm not afraid of pain."

"That's what they all say," Lyle assured her, "at first."

Gage's claws were out. He wanted to rip into that bastard. He *would*. As soon as that gun wasn't pointed at Kayla's head.

Kayla walked from the cage. Because of the chain that bound them, Gage had to step forward, too. Slowly, carefully.

"Stop right there, Gage, that's far enough," Lyle commanded and Gage caught the scent of the bastard's sweat. Good. Lyle was afraid. He should be.

As Gage stared at him, Lyle's left hand lowered and came back up with a set of keys. But his right hand—the bastard lifted his right hand and pressed the barrel of the gun between Kayla's eyes. "Now be a good girl," he directed, "and unlock your handcuff. Then drop the chain."

Kayla's fingers were rock steady as she reached for the keys. Gage couldn't see her face, just the perfectly straight line of her back. He hated the sight of that gun barrel pressed against her head. Hated—

Lyle pulled the trigger.

Chapter Six

THE SHIFT HIT GAGE INSTANTLY. A WILD BURST OF fiery pain ignited within him as the wolf inside erupted in fury. He fell to the ground, landing on all fours, and his hands began to twist into claws. The man couldn't control the beast this time.

Gun. Kayla. Shot.

There was too much fury. Too much pain and rage.

Lyle's laughter echoed in his ears. "Don't worry, the first chamber was empty."

Gage managed to lift his head. The man he'd been was slipping away. Too much hate burned inside of him.

Lyle could have killed her.

"The second one, though, it's not empty," Lyle promised. "So stay in the cage, wolf, or you really will watch me blow her brains out."

The silver chain burned against his flesh. Burned even hotter now that the wolf was coming out, but the shift was exactly what he needed to lose the cuff that circled his wrist. Because he didn't have a human wrist anymore. The bones snapped. Elongated. Became narrow enough to slide from that silver cuff, and, sure enough, the cuff fell from his paw a few seconds later. The lock on Kayla's cuffs clicked open. She caught the chain, not letting it fall to the stone floor.

Lyle looked back at him. "I knew the beast wanted her."

More than he wanted breath.

"So I figured I'd see just how much control the man had over—*Ah!*" Lyle's words ended in a scream. Kayla had jerked the chain back toward her. Since it wasn't anchored to Gage anymore, it flew easily into her grip. Then she slammed that silver right at Lyle. Right into the bastard's face. The gun fell from Lyle's hands. A bullet fired out and slammed into the side of the cage's bars.

The scent of smoking flesh filled Gage's nostrils.

And since the cage door was conveniently open, the wolf just leapt right out of the prison.

Kayla kicked out with her foot and sent Lyle stumbling to the floor. Then she jumped on top of him and wrapped the silver chain around his neck. Once. Twice. "You're gonna play Russian roulette with me?" Kayla snarled. "I don't think so, you bastard!"

Lyle tossed her away. She flew back, and her body crashed into the side of the cage.

Lyle grabbed at the chain, and the silver burned his fingers. *Your turn to enjoy the pain, asshole.* Before the guy could get free, Gage was on him. His claws dug into Lyle's chest as he penned the bastard to the floor.

Then Gage lowered his head for the kill.

Lyle started laughing again. "D-do it," he dared, and Lyle's face was showing the pressure of his own impending shift. The guy's wolf wanted out. It was there to see, in the bright eyes, the hollowed cheeks, and the lengthening canines. "Do it and her—her brother's dead."

Like a human was really supposed to matter to him. A human who'd *shot* Kayla.

Gage's teeth sank into Lyle's throat.

And Kayla's hands closed around the back of Gage's head. She yanked on him, trying to pull him up. What? Was the woman crazy? You didn't grab a wolf by the head. She jumped back when he came up snarling.

Then she grabbed him by the tail.

The fuck, *no*.

"Please," she begged him, voice strained and desperate. "Let's just make sure my brother's safe first, then we can kill him, okay?"

No, that was not *okay*. He wanted Lyle dead right then and there.

Kayla hurriedly backed away. He'd expected her to keep fighting.

Blood dripped down Lyle's face. "Y-you're so...fucked!"

Said the man who was about to lose his throat.

"I'm...already in...your pack."

Right, Gage knew that shit. Betrayal was a bitter, burning pill to swallow. But he'd suspected the truth. A wolf, one of his own, had sold him and the pack out to the hunters.

To this wolf in a damn hunter's guise.

Who is it? The demand of the man inside the beast. Only the beast couldn't speak. He had to shift back in order to manage that. But...

But he heard the sound of racing footsteps just outside the door. The holding room might not have audio surveillance, but the hunters patrolling the area hadn't missed the sound of a gunshot. They weren't that clueless.

And speaking of that gun...

Kayla was back at his side. *Now her retreat made sense.*

She'd gone for the weapon. Kayla aimed the gun at Lyle's head. Payback. She was a sexy bitch.

"Where's my brother?" Kayla demanded.

Gage kept Lyle penned. Kept that bastard bleeding as he let his claws sink even deeper into his flesh.

Lyle spat blood. "Getting...sliced open!"

She fired the gun. The bullet sank into Lyle's right shoulder. The shifter howled in pain and rage.

"My bad," Kayla murmured. "I thought that chamber would be empty."

Before Lyle could do more than growl in pain, the door of the holding room flew open.

Gage glanced up. *Huh. Guess we found her brother.*

Because Gage was staring straight into eyes the same golden shade as Kayla's. The man's hair was curly and dark, just like hers, but his face was harder. All lines and stark angles.

The guy was wearing black, shoulder to damn toe, and he was armed.

More men rushed in after Jonah. All wearing black like it was some sort of hunter uniform, probably because it was. All of them were holding weapons. Weapons they aimed at him and Kayla.

"Shoot them!" Lyle screamed as he bucked beneath Gage's hold. "The bitch is...helping him! They're trying to escape!"

And that was why Kayla should have let him kill the prick when he'd had the chance. Now at least six weapons were pointed at him and Kayla. Not the best odds. But he'd had worse.

"Don't anyone fucking fire at Kayla!" That was her brother roaring that order. Would the others actually listen? Right then, they all looked confused. A little scared, too.

Maybe they hadn't faced off against too many shifted wolves before.

Sometimes, the hunting was easier to do from a distance. When you got up close and personal with a wolf, fear could slip past any man's guard.

"Jonah!" Kayla cried out her brother's name and tried to rush toward the hunter.

Gage leapt forward and put his body between her and the armed men. Had the woman missed the guns? He opened up his mouth and snarled a warning at her—and them. *Stay the hell back.*

"Shoot the bastard!" Lyle yelled. It sounded like the prick was getting stronger. Shifters always healed fast.

"My pleasure," Jonah said with a slow, mean grin.

"No! Dammit, *don't!*" Kayla was screaming now. Her voice shook with fury as she threatened, "If you shoot Gage, I'll put a bullet in Lyle's head!" Then she scrambled back. Scrambled back—and pressed the gun barrel to Lyle's head. If the hunters had just arrived five minutes sooner, they would have seen their boss toying with her. Getting off on her fear.

But now, they just saw Kayla. Threatening to kill the man they all probably idolized. Dumbasses.

"Kayla." Sorrow whispered through her name as Jonah spoke. "You can't do this." The faint lines around his eyes deepened. "You can't!"

"He's a shifter!" Kayla snapped back at him. "Lyle's a wolf! He's been lying to us all for years! Haven't you ever wondered why he didn't go into any of the interrogations with the other shifters? It's because they would have known what he was! They would have—"

"She's crazy," Lyle tossed right back as spittle flew from his mouth. "She's screwing that shifter, and she's lying to-to try and save…his ass! They broke…out of the cage and tried to…kill me!"

Who were the hunters going to believe? Their boss? Or the woman who'd just shot Lyle? Gage didn't wait for their reaction. He attacked.

The first swipe of his claws went toward her brother. *Shouldn't have shot her.* He sliced deep into the guy's arm, and Jonah stumbled back.

Kayla's scream grated in his ears. He hated the sound of her pain. But he couldn't stop, not now.

A bullet sank into his side. Asshole hunters. He clawed the nearest one. Slammed his head into the legs of another. Used his teeth to take down a third.

"Told you!" Lyle shouted. The guy's voice was *definitely* stronger now. "I told you he was a killer! Twisted, sick son of a bitch. Take him out!"

A gun blast destroyed the last of his words.

Gage whirled around. He saw Lyle groaning. Grabbing his leg.

This time, Kayla had shot Lyle in the upper thigh.

"That'll slow you down," she snapped. Then she looked up at Gage. Her gaze burned with fury. So much rage.

Directed at me. So he'd made her brother bleed. The dick had deserved it.

An alarm sounded somewhere down the hall. No doubt, more hunters would be there soon in response to that shrill cry. Over-eager men and women who couldn't wait to pump his body full of silver.

They had to get out of there before the backup arrived.

Kayla hurried to her brother's side while Lyle continued to scream.

"Jonah?"

Her brother's head had slammed into the stone wall,

courtesy of Gage. He vaguely remembered shoving Jonah back after he'd clawed into him. Jonah's right hand bled. The muscles near his wrist had been slashed deep.

Jonah was trying to stop the blood flow, but his shirt was already stained red. "Why?" Jonah rasped. "Why...for him?"

She put her hands over his wound. "It's going to be all right. I promise, everything will—"

"It will never be okay, sis...*never*."

Gage rushed toward her. They had to leave, *now*. Still in wolf form, his head pushed against her shoulder.

She shoved him back. "Get out of here, Gage."

That screeching alarm hurt his ears. And it must have messed up his hearing because there was no way she'd just said—

She yanked at her shirt, ripping the material, and wrapped it around her brother's wrist. "He's going to bleed out if I can't get this stopped!"

Were those tears in her eyes? The wound wasn't that bad. She just needed to take a breath and see that. If he'd wanted, he could have made the dumbass lose his whole arm.

I just gave him something to remember me by.

He closed his teeth around her wrist. Pulled lightly.

She shook her head. "*Go!* I'm not leaving. I *can't* leave him."

But he was supposed to just turn tail and leave his mate behind?

"Stop them!" Lyle was shouting again. Hell. Could this shit get any more screwed?

"Go," she told Gage again, and dammit, those *were* tears. He hated the sight of them.

More hunters were coming. Gage could smell their

sweat. Excitement and fear. They'd come in, and he'd attack.

They'd shoot.

Who would survive?

Get to the pack. There was a traitor in their midst. As alpha, it was his job to keep them safe.

Even if it meant leaving his mate behind?

Kayla's gaze held his.

No more time.

The wolf turned away from her and leapt through the doorway. He raced down the hallway, using his enhanced senses to guide him. Fresh air and freedom to the left. More containment rooms and prisoners to the right. Guards coming in fast.

He dodged, leapt—and flew straight through the window. Glass rained around him and when he landed outside on the dank earth, Gage didn't look back.

Even though he knew the hunters were giving chase.

Fools. Didn't they know that in this hunt, they'd be the prey?

* * *

No one listened to her. She tried to tell Jonah the truth about Lyle. She tried to tell the other hunters.

They'd ignored her.

Cuffed her.

Tossed her into another cell.

Dammit.

Jonah had been taken away. Rushed to the med unit. He'd be okay. *He'd be okay.* They'd stop the bleeding and her brother would survive. There just wasn't an alternative for him—or her.

Gage had attacked Jonah. She should have expected that move. You weren't supposed to trust wolves. Everyone knew they had a tendency to bite the hand that fed them.

Like he'd nearly bitten off her brother's hand.

A guard came inside the holding area. Curtis Latham. She knew him. Curtis was new but she'd worked with him in the field once. Saved his ass that day, too. The man had *better* remember that. Kayla ran toward the cell door. "I'm telling the truth!" Telling it to anyone who'd listen, only no one would believe her. "Go check Lyle's wounds. He's *burned* because I used silver on him."

Curtis narrowed his gaze on her. "You shot him. Twice."

True. Was she supposed to be sorry for that? "He put his gun to my head and pulled the trigger. He's a sick SOB that needs to be put down."

Curtis glanced away. "He's the reason I'm still alive."

Yes, well, she'd thought the same thing, not too long ago. Then she'd learned the terrible truth. "He's lying to you. To us all! Please, Curtis, just go and check his wounds." Before Lyle healed himself.

Curtis glanced back at her. His eyes were confused. Angry. "He said for me to guard you."

She grabbed the bars and jerked on them. "Where am I supposed to go? I'm in a cell!" Kayla all but screamed at him. "Just go look at Lyle. His neck and his hands. The silver burned him. He's a wolf, I swear!"

A muscle jerked along Curtis's jaw. Then he slowly shook his head. "Lyle's the one who gave the order—he wants you to stay alive. If he'd really tried to kill you, then why would he do that?"

So that he could use her later. But that wasn't going to happen. Her time being bait was over. Didn't Lyle get that?

Gage was gone. He knew the full deal about her—about all the hunters. He'd escaped the grounds, and he wasn't coming back. Not for her.

Not for anything.

"I've fought with you," she told Curtis and knew that desperation threaded through her words. "Stood by your side. Covered your back. And I've never lied to you." She just had to make him listen. "Please, check his wounds. All you have to do is look at his hands and neck!"

The holding room door opened. Lyle walked in, limping heavily Her gaze immediately went to his neck and—*healed.* No burns.

Bastard. Damn quick-healing wolf.

Lyle smiled at her, then winced, lifting his hand to his shoulder. She could see the bandages clearly. What a load of bull. If his burns had healed, then that bullet wound had healed, too. He was just playing a game in front of Curtis and the other hunters.

"Boss, you okay?" Curtis asked at once.

Kayla rolled her eyes. "Of course, he is. The guy's a wolf, he can heal from almost anything."

"Is she still screaming that story about me being an animal?" Lyle's steps were slow, as if he were hurt. He kept dragging his "injured" leg. Now that she knew the truth about him, Lyle's acting skills were pretty impressive. He'd sure fooled her for years.

Why can't anyone see through the lies? Why couldn't I?

Maybe people just saw what they wanted to see. No, what they *needed* to see?

And what had she needed to see? A hero. A man who'd saved her from the wolves. A friend who wanted to protect her and make her stronger.

Not a lying killer who'd just wanted to use her.

"Someone had to see your wounds," she told him. "Not just the bullet wounds—the burn wounds from the silver." There'd been too many other hunters in that holding room. *Someone* would have noticed his burns. "All your lies are about to come out."

Curtis glanced nervously between them. "Boss...I, uh, I thought I saw some blisters on you earlier."

"She'd been punching me. My skin was red from her attack." Lyle gave a little shrug with his "uninjured" shoulder. "I'll probably bruise later."

"Bullshit," Kayla called.

Curtis shifted from one foot to the other. "I-I know the difference between blisters and punch marks." He peered at Lyle's neck again. *Yes. He was getting suspicious.*

"Pull back his bandage!" Kayla urged. This would do it. "Check out the bullet wound at his shoulder, because I bet it's already healed, too." Curtis was starting to believe her. This would work. She'd get out of there and together, she and Curtis could take Lyle down.

"You're so desperate," Lyle said, sighing, as a frown pulled down his mouth. "When did you become like this? Did Gage make you this way?"

If Lyle had been just a few feet closer to the cell, she would have attacked. But he wasn't heading toward her. Instead, Lyle was closing the distance between him and Curtis.

"I don't want you to doubt me," Lyle told the hunter. He wasn't wearing a shirt. Just a heavy white bandage around his shoulder. A loose pair of sweat pants. "If this is what it takes to prove the truth to you, then so be it." His hands rose to the bandage.

Curtis nodded. He leaned forward. "I just need to know —Kayla's always been so—"

Lyle grabbed him by the head.

Kayla screamed.

And Lyle broke Curtis's neck with one powerful twist of his hand. The hunter never even had a chance to cry out.

Lyle let Curtis's body drop to the floor. Curtis hit with a thud. Shaking his head, Lyle stared down at the hunter's twisted body. "You shouldn't have doubted me, kid."

Ice filled Kayla's veins. Horror and nausea spun in her gut, and she could taste bile rising in her throat. *Dead.* "You bastard—*why?*"

He looked up at her. Frowned. "It's your fault that he's dead. You should have just kept your damn mouth shut, and he'd still be breathing."

Only Curtis wasn't breathing. He was dead. And how many more would fall before Lyle was done?

How many had he killed over the years? When she'd thought that the hunters had been protecting humans, fighting the monsters...

Oh, God, we were the monsters.

Lyle grabbed the body and dragged Curtis's limp form over to the cell. Lyle dropped him near the bars. "There. When the body's discovered, everyone will just think you killed him. Curtis got too close, and you attacked him. We all know how lethal you can be."

Her hands wouldn't stop shaking. *She* couldn't stop shaking. Tears burned her eyes.

"He got too close, trusted the wrong person, and you snapped his neck." Lyle snapped his fingers. "Just like that."

Her knees wanted to give way. She stood only because of her desperate grip on the bars. "What do you want from me?" *Curtis. Dead.*

"I want your wolf."

She shook her head. "He's gone. Gage isn't coming back."

Lyle smiled. "We'll see about that." Then he turned away and headed back toward the holding room door. Was that psycho actually whistling as he walked away and left her with a dead body?

"Gage chose his pack!" Kayla cried after him. "Not me. That's why he left! He went to keep them safe." Gage wasn't coming back.

Lyle glanced over his shoulder. "Then I guess you'll be the next one to die."

When he left, the metal clang of the door seemed to echo through the whole room. Through her. She looked over at Curtis. So still. His eyes were closed, his head turned toward her.

He'd been a good man. He hadn't deserved this end.

She let go of the bars, and her knees buckled. She slipped to the floor and her fingers, still stained with her brother's blood, rose to cover her eyes.

We're the monsters.

Why hadn't she seen the truth sooner?

Gage tracked silently through the compound. He knew where Kayla was, of course. Her scent was one he'd never forget. So he eased through the hallways, slipped around the corners, and tracked back to her as quickly as he could.

Outside of her new holding room, he paused. Inhaled. Kayla wasn't alone in there. But the one with her...

Shit.

Gage used the key card he'd "borrowed" from the guard

station and swiped it across the electronic lock. The lights flashed green, and he shoved open the heavy, metal door.

Kayla was in the cell, on the floor. Her hair fell in a curtain around her. A hunter was slumped close to her. His neck was twisted, and his hands were stretched out on either side of his body.

"I didn't do it," she said, without looking up. "I swear, I didn't kill Curtis."

"Sweetheart, you don't have to tell me that."

Her head whipped up. Her eyes widened. "You—you shouldn't be here!"

He glanced back down at the unmoving body. "There's something you should realize, though." He made sure the door was shut behind him. "Curtis isn't dead."

Chapter Seven

Gage advanced slowly, letting his claws rip from his fingertips. The guy smelled human. Well, mostly. But he didn't have the stench of death about him, and usually, that scent came quickly once the heart stopped beating.

Gage put his hand out on the man's chest. No heartbeat. That *should* have meant the fellow was dead. But with the supernaturals, *should* didn't really apply so much.

Then the one she'd called Curtis sucked in a sharp breath. His eyes flew open, and beneath Gage's hand, his heart started to beat once more.

Sonofabitch.

Gage had never seen anything quite like that.

Then Curtis's head and neck snapped back in place.

"Oh, my God." Kayla's whisper.

"Not quite," the guy said, and his eyes—the eyes that still held Gage's—changed. The blue color faded until only black remained. "But I have heard that demons are distantly related to angels, so who the hell really knows?"

Demons.

And that was exactly the type of being that Gage was staring at.

Curtis glanced at Gage's hands. "I really hope you aren't planning to use those claws on me. Especially since I was gonna help you out."

"You're a demon?" Kayla asked. She was back on her feet now. "What the hell? A demon hunter at my side and a shifter for a boss? Are there any humans other than me and Jonah in this place?"

Curtis shrugged. "Probably." He lifted a brow at Gage. "Uh, those claws?"

Gage backed off, for the moment.

Curtis took another deep breath. "Thanks. I'd prefer to die only once today."

"Only you didn't die!" Kayla snapped back. "Dammit, I was *crying* over you."

"And that was really sweet," Curtis retorted instantly. "I was touched that you cared about me."

She tried to grab him through the cage bars.

He leapt away and jumped quickly to his feet. "I *had* to play dead, okay? What? You think I was gonna take him on? I'm a low-level demon. He's a shifter. If he'd found out what I actually was, the jerk would have just sliced off my head."

That was a fast way to kill a demon.

"Broken bones are nothing." Curtis sighed. "I've always had a special knack for healing them. Guess that's my main talent. But there's no coming back once you actually lose your head."

Not for any supernatural. Beheading would pretty much kill them all.

"I was just waiting for Lyle to clear out," Curtis added, voice reeking of sincerity as he faced Kayla. "I had to be sure he was gone, then I was going to let you know I was all right. I was just about to move when *he* pushed open the door."

"Get. Me. Out." Kayla gritted. Her cheeks were flushed. Her eyes sharp, golden glass.

Curtis yanked his keys from his pocket and fumbled to free her. The second that door opened, Curtis tried to scurry back. Too late.

Kayla slugged him. Damn. That was a powerful right hook. Good thing the demon could heal so fast.

"Don't ever make me think you're dead again!" Kayla raged at him.

"Ow! Shit, I was trying to help!" Curtis rubbed his jaw. "I was waiting for the coast to clear, then I was gonna help you get out."

"And you still will," Gage assured him. He didn't know what the demon was doing working there as a hunter, and right then, he didn't give a shit. He just wanted to get Kayla out of that place.

He had to hurry up and go check in on his pack. Once they were secure, and once he'd destroyed the fool who'd betrayed him to Lyle, then he could come back and bring this compound to the ground.

Curtis nodded. "Right. I-I still will."

"We need transportation," Gage said. Number one priority. They were in the middle of the desert. They needed a fast ride. One that wouldn't be traced.

"There are a fleet of SUVs in this place. I can handle getting transport." Curtis nodded and rocked back on his heels. "But I'm going with you."

Like he wanted another hunter riding shotgun.

Before he could refuse, Kayla nodded. Her eyes met Gage's. "If he stays, he really will be dead."

She kept acting like he was supposed to care about the

hunters. But...*fine.* Gage pointed at Curtis. "Demon, I don't trust you."

"Fair enough," Curtis returned instantly. The demon was sweating. "I don't trust wolves, either. One just tried to kill me."

The demon was a dick.

Curtis grinned. "Want to know why I'm a hunter?"

"Because you're a screwed up demon?" Gage tossed back as he scanned the area. No cameras in the room. No audio surveillance. Lyle had probably ditched everything so he could speak freely with Kayla. Good. They were clear. *Let's haul ass.*

"I'm a hunter because two years ago, a wolf shifter killed my mother. A shifter I've spent months tracking."

Curtis was staring at him a little too intently. "I didn't kill your mother." Gage hadn't killed a demon in at least three years, not two. And he sure hadn't killed any women. He had a rule about that.

"She wasn't a demon. She was human." Sadness whispered through Curtis's words.

So the guy wasn't a full demon. A hybrid. That explained the human scent that clung to him—and that had to be the reason why he'd managed to fool Lyle.

Gage had an enhanced sense of smell, even among wolves. But Lyle—that SOB might not have been able to pick up on the slight difference in Curtis's scent.

Lucky for the demon or else he would have gotten a broken neck much, much sooner.

Or maybe that beheading.

Curtis told him, "Lyle found her body, or so he said. And he promised that he'd help me track her killer."

Only Gage figured that Lyle *had* been the killer.

"He promised me that, too," Kayla whispered. "He swore we'd stop the wolf who'd hurt my family."

"I can't forget her," Curtis said and the pain hardened his voice. "Her throat was sliced open. He'd...clawed her. Torn her open. I-I just wanted to find the shifter and *make him pay*."

Rage was something Gage could understand. So was vengeance.

Kayla's glittering stare told him that she understood just as well.

"Don't worry," Gage promised as they headed for the door. *Get out. Get the pack safe. Then destroy.* "We'll make the bastard suffer." They'd make him burn.

KAYLA KNEW they couldn't leave. Several SUVs were there, just about twenty feet away. Riding off in one would be the perfect escape. But...

But she couldn't do it.

Jonah. Dammit, there had been so much blood pouring from his wound. Was her brother okay?

Did Gage really think that she was just going to race out of the compound and leave him behind?

Leave Jonah and the others?

I can't get to Jonah while he's in the med unit. There'd be too many eyes and ears on him in that place. But while Jonah and the other hunters were getting stitched up...*We can save the wolves.*

"They're in containment," she softly revealed to Gage. She wasn't looking at him yet because she was still plenty furious. *He'd hurt her brother.*

Gage would pay for that, but now wasn't the time to go

at him for her pound of flesh. Now was the time for fast action.

Curtis wasn't with them. He was preparing for their big escape.

Crouching, staying low behind a line of boxes, Gage turned to look at her. "What? Who's in containment?"

The breath she sucked in felt cold in her lungs. *We're the monsters*. Time to be something else. Better. "Your wolves aren't dead." She wasn't a cold-blooded killer. Neither were the other hunters. They were doing their jobs. Or what they *thought* had been their jobs. "They're in containment at this facility. I don't—I don't think they've been transferred out yet."

Shipped out to a far more secure location—one that no one had escaped from since she'd been in Vegas. The hunters weren't just attacking supernaturals blindly. They had a hit list. Of sorts.

Most of their orders came from Lyle, but he was on a leash, too. Or at least, she'd always thought he had been. The hunters were tied to good old Uncle Sam—or maybe not-so-good Uncle Sam. The government sent them out on missions that normal channels just couldn't cover.

When they caught their prey, the hunters turned them over to the federal agents for holding. Or for extermination. So the story went. Only now she wondered just how many "exterminations" had truly been necessary?

Her gut clenched. How much blood was on her hands? And could she ever get it the hell off? She was afraid that no matter how hard she scrubbed, the stain would always remain.

"We can get them out," Kayla said. They had to get them out. Now that she knew the truth about Lyle, leaving the two wolves behind wasn't an option for her.

"We just have to move fast." Before Lyle realized that Curtis wasn't dead and that she wasn't still locked in her own cage.

Gage's gaze hardened. "When were you gonna tell me they were still alive?"

"Uh, now?" Okay, yes, she should have mentioned it earlier. Would have if it hadn't been for the whole drugging and gun-in-her face thing. Jeez. She was doing her best.

"Both of them?" Gage bit out. "Shamus and Faye?"

"Yes." And, well, they'd been mostly all right when she last saw them.

Before she'd headed out to say her "I do" with Gage, Lyle had told her that the wolves weren't due for transport for another two days. So as long as those plans hadn't changed, "They'll be in Block B." Sequestered. Monitored. Getting inside that area would be tricky, but they could do it.

She wanted this blood off her hands.

Curtis hadn't returned yet. If they were going, they needed to move, *now*. They'd get the shifters, then haul ass back for their getaway SUV. If luck was on her side—*yeah, right, since when?*—they'd bust out of this place before any trigger-happy hunters could spot them.

"Come on." She barely breathed the words. She had her hair shoved under a black cap and she'd donned the black uniform of a hunter, just like Gage. The better to try and blend in with everyone else. That blending would last only for so long.

But most of the hunters were in the infirmary or out on a mission. Only a skeleton staff walked the hallways and with Gage's enhanced senses, they would be able to dodge those people easily enough.

He always knew when someone was coming. From

what she could tell, Gage seemed to smell the hunters long before she heard them. Such a handy talent.

He nodded, and the hunt started.

Adrenaline raced through her blood, keeping her tense and edgy. But this wasn't her first op, and she knew how to hold on to her control. They crept soundlessly down the stairs that led to Block B. The transport area. The prisoners housed in Block B were all due to ship off for continued confinement.

The only ones housed there now were the wolves. Category H—for Hostile Holding. "We have to take out the surveillance first," Kayla whispered. Her hands were sweating. Her heart beating so quickly. Escape had been at hand, but now they were in the belly of the beast again. All by her choice.

You owe the shifters. Do this.

The door to the surveillance room was shut. Her fingers lifted and punched in the access code. Lyle wouldn't have been able to reprogram all the access codes, not yet. At least, she *hoped* he hadn't.

The lights flashed green. *Yes.* She shoved open the door.

The hunter watching the monitors for Block B spun toward her in surprise. "Kayla? Why are you—"

Gage lifted his gun. "Don't move," he ordered as he stalked toward the blond male.

The hunter froze. "K-Kayla? What's going on?"

"I'm sorry, Thomas, but those prisoners aren't being transferred."

Gage was less than a foot from Thomas now. Could Thomas see the flash of fang? Probably. He was sweating. Trying to back up and—

Gage grabbed him and rammed the Thomas's head into the wall. One hard rap, and Thomas fell.

Hell. Kayla raced across the room. "You weren't supposed to hurt him!"

"And he wasn't supposed to have shifter blood beneath his nails." Gage's nostrils flared, and she knew he was pulling in the scent. His jaw tight, he growled, "The bastard's lucky that he's still breathing."

He *was* still breathing. But Thomas was definitely out.

Gage's gaze rose to the monitors. "Shamus."

She stood slowly and followed his stare. He was looking at the redheaded male wolf shifter who had been brought in first for containment. She still didn't know how an Irish wolf had wound up in the new Vegas pack, and from what she'd gathered, Shamus hadn't exactly been the sharing sort.

Blood dripped from the redhead's side. He stood just a foot away from the silver bars, and he glared straight up at the camera.

Shamus had put two hunters in the infirmary when he'd been brought in.

An animal. Lyle's words drifted through her mind. *See how wild? How vicious? This one will have to be put down before he can kill again.*

"Has he killed?" Kayla asked quietly.

Gage nodded.

So have I. When had the line between good and evil become so blurry? Maybe it had just always been that way. "Has he killed innocents?" she pressed.

Gage's stare slowly turned to her. "I'm getting him out of there."

Okay, so that wasn't the answer she'd been hoping to hear. Kayla grabbed his arm and stopped him. "If that wolf is gonna get loose, then turn on humans, I can't let that happen." That would just be more death on her. Kayla swallowed. "I've seen what wolf shifters can do to humans. I won't let him hurt innocent people like that."

Gage stared down at her. "When will you stop judging us all, based on what happened to you?"

She felt that hit all the way to her soul. But Kayla didn't let him go. "Is he a threat to humans?" Lyle had said so, but now she knew Lyle was a lying sack of shit.

That I trusted for years. That I freaking loved. He'd been a second father to her, only the increasing icy certainty in her gut told her that the creep had quite possibly killed her real father.

No, not quite possibly. *You did it. I know you did.* Her blinders had been smashed to pieces now.

And I was with Lyle. I fought side by side with him for years and didn't realize the truth.

She had to clench her teeth to hold back the scream that wanted to break free. She'd been so blind. So driven by rage and anger. Lyle had given her targets, and she'd been only too eager to attack.

"I trust Shamus." Gage spoke softly to her. His body was tense beneath her hand. "Things haven't been easy for him. But he isn't psychotic."

As wolves were prone to be. *Like you, Lyle?*

"He's in control, and as far as I know, Shamus never killed a human in his life, not even those who deserved death."

Her breath rushed out. Okay, that was something.

"And the woman?" The female wolf. The one with the short, close-cropped black hair, the tawny skin, and the dark eyes that looked like she'd seen hell a time or twenty.

"Faye can't shift."

That surprised her. "She's a hybrid?" Kayla had heard

about another wolf like that, once, but that wolf shifter had lived way down south.

"No. She's full-blooded." His gaze darted to the screen that showed Faye's image. "But when she was thirteen, a sick prick got hold of her. A doctor who said he could cure wolves. Faye's parents wanted her cured."

"Why?" She'd thought wolves loved their beasts.

"Because they didn't want to be monsters. Didn't want her to be one."

Kayla flinched.

"The doctor pumped liquid silver in her veins. Burned her from the inside out. She's never been able to change."

Her eyes squeezed shut. She couldn't even guess the agony a procedure like that would bring to a child. "What happened to the doctor?"

"The human who got off on torturing wolves?" Fury burned in his voice. "Don't worry. He's not 'curing' anyone. Not anymore."

No. She bet he wasn't.

Not good. Not evil.

Where did Gage really fall on that scale? Where did she?

Her eyes opened. Determination fueled her blood. "Let's get them out of there before the next guard shift comes to check on Thomas."

She grabbed the key cards. Headed for the woman first. Faye stood in the middle of her prison. Her head was down. Her body held perfectly still.

But when Kayla and Gage entered the narrow corridor that led toward the caged wolf, the woman's body tensed. Her head snapped back. *"Alpha."* Hope and fear twisted the one word.

Gage hurried toward her. "We're getting you out, Faye."

Faye's dark gaze—her eyes almost looked pitch black—locked on Kayla. "The hunter? She...smells of you."

Great. Shifter noses. Kayla swiped the key card and jerked open the cell door. "Come on."

One wolf down.

One to go.

But Faye didn't move. Her gaze stayed locked on Kayla. "Is this...a trick?" she asked. Her eyes narrowed. "You hate me. Why would you help us?" That gaze slid back to Gage. "Even if you're fucking the alpha,"

Yeah, I am fucking him. And with shifter senses, well, hell, she might as well be wearing a giant neon sign that said, *Hi, I'm Kayla, and I just screwed the alpha.*

"Why go against your own kind?" Faye demanded and her soft voice was laced with steely anger.

"Because they're not my kind." Lyle wasn't. He wasn't Gage's kind, either. He was just a murdering, sick bastard. *That* kind.

He'd told them all that Faye was psychotic. That she'd sliced open five men in Vegas. Kayla had seen the pictures, but hadn't talked to the men. Lyle had told her interviews weren't necessary. Now she needed to hear Faye's side of the story. "Why'd you do it?"

Faye held up her hand. Claws broke from her fingertips. "The bastard doctor didn't totally kill my wolf."

Were the claws supposed to scare her? *Think again.* "Five men are now walking the streets of Vegas with your mark on their faces. *Why?*"

Because Kayla had to make sure she was doing the right thing. She was going against years of training. Everything she'd ever believed.

Faye's delicate face hardened. "Those *men*," the word was a curse, "got off on hurting women, and they made the mistake of thinking they'd hurt me, too." Faye's lips thinned. "No one hurts me and just walks away. Those days are long gone."

There was no missing Faye's intensity. Or the pain that echoed in her voice. Kayla stared at her—and believed Faye's words.

Not evil. Not good.

Was the whole world a shade of gray? Everything had seemed to be in such big, bold colors just days before.

Kayla turned away from Faye. Staring into the she-wolf's eyes, it was a little too much like...*looking in a mirror.*

Same rage. Same pain.

"Alpha?" Faye's hesitant voice. "Shamus...I heard him yelling...is he...?"

"He's next," Gage replied, voice flat. "You're both coming home."

Home. The word caused an ache to lodge in Kayla's heart. Did she even have one anymore?

Don't think about it. Not now. She just needed to do the job. Get them all out of there with minimum bloodshed, yeah, that was priority number one for her. She slipped around the corner, punched in the code for the next holding room, and tried like hell to keep her control in place.

Time to face the big beast. Shamus would hear her coming, no doubt, but it wasn't him she was worried about. Well, not *too* worried. Not with Gage having her back.

We just have to hurry.

Lyle was too confident. He thought the silver was all he needed to contain his captured prey.

Guess you never thought one of your own would turn on you.

Time for Lyle to think again.

"Come near me and I'll cut you open!" Shamus

bellowed and she flinched. *Hell, did he have to yell?* Did he want to bring all the other guards his way?

Actually, getting cut open by him was pretty likely. So she'd better stay far away from those razor-sharp claws.

"I'm trying to help you," she muttered as she rounded one more turn and came face-to-face with his cage and him.

Big Red was freaking huge. Had to be at least six-foot-three, maybe six-foot-four. His shoulders were like dang mountains.

"If you so much as scratch her, Shamus, you'll answer to me," Gage snarled from directly behind her. *Soft moving wolf.*

Silence. Shamus's stare drifted between them. "A hunter?" Disgust dripped from the words.

"I'm the hunter who's here to save your ass." She used the key card, and his cell door swung open.

Shamus didn't move. "Is this a trick?" His claws were up. Before Kayla could answer, he lunged forward—and those claws came right at her neck.

She jumped back, but Gage was already there. He leapt in front of her and locked his hand around Shamus's thick throat and slammed him back against the silver bars.

Faye cried out as the scent of burning flesh filled the air.

"I *warned* you," Gage growled. Then he yanked Shamus away from the bars and dropped him on the floor. "She's mine, and you *don't* ever go at her with your claws. Got it?"

Shamus lifted his head. "G-got...it, alpha."

Right. When a lesson was burned into you, it was kinda hard to misunderstand.

Psychotic tendencies. That had been in Shamus's file. His gaze cut to her. Oh, yes, white-hot fury and—

"Faye," Shamus whispered the woman's name like a

prayer. The fury vanished from his eyes and was replaced by a look of longing so intense that Kayla felt damn uncomfortable.

Faye had crept near her. Then the smaller woman paused, and rocked nervously from one foot to the other.

"I caught your scent on the hunter," Shamus said. He rose to his feet in an instant and didn't even seem to be aware that his back was still smoking. "I-I thought he'd done something to you, that—"

"*Later.*" Gage's snarl but through Shamus's words. "We're getting the hell out of here now."

Kayla got the picture. Big Red was sweet on not-so-delicate Faye. But Faye wasn't even looking at him. She was looking *everywhere* else. The cage. The ceiling. The floor. The floor had to be real fascinating the way she was staring so hard at it.

Shamus had been captured when he'd charged at the hunters—coming straight in for a direct attack against them.

"You came at us because we had her," Kayla said, understanding now. That was almost sweet.

Shamus threw her a fast glance. Wow, wait, his cheeks had just heated. He didn't look quite so fierce in that instance.

Gage caught her hand. "There's movement two hallways over. Guards."

Crap. Okay, the weird love thing between the wolves could wait.

She pulled out her weapon. She'd taken the liberty of snagging it when she'd taken the uniform from the locker room. "I'll get us back to Curtis." Then she'd leave Gage because her work wasn't done. Not yet. "You just stop me if you hear guards, or if you smell them."

No way would she walk into an ambush. Not with her wolf by her side.

Her wolf? Now she was definitely getting all possessive on him. She was in such trouble.

Gage stopped her twice as they headed back to the garage. She knew he could have just killed the guards they passed. Knew that Shamus wanted to slice them open, but Faye's light touch on his arm seemed to calm the big wolf. Right then, they were all focused on escape. But judging by the glint in Gage's eyes, the fight would come soon enough.

She just wondered how many lives would be lost when the hunters faced off against the whole Vegas wolf pack.

Not Jonah. She'd have to make sure he didn't get caught in the crossfire.

Though it seemed to take forever, they were soon back in the shadows of the garage. When it came to stealth, no one beat the wolves. Just get them away from silver, and they were good to go.

Lethally good.

"How the hell are we getting out of here?" Shamus wanted to know. "There's a fortified fence out there, patrolled with half a dozen armed guards."

Once you got in, you weren't supposed to get out. Unless you were a hunter.

Curtis stood next to one of the compound's SUVs. He was rocking back and forth as nervous energy seemed to roll from him.

Could the wolves smell him sweating?

"You're just gonna drive out," Kayla told Shamus and, from the corner of her eye, she saw Gage's head snap toward her. "Easy as pie." Not exactly. She glanced at Gage and found herself caught in his stare.

"*We're* gonna drive out," he corrected.

Right, ahem, he would have caught that bit.

But now wasn't the time to hash this mess out. Curtis had seen her, and he lifted his hand, indicating the coast was clear. They hauled ass, staying low and in the shadows, as they headed for the vehicle. Shamus and Faye jumped in the backseat and kept their bodies near the floorboard. For such a big guy, Shamus could sure cram in tight. If anyone looked over, they wouldn't even see those two in the back.

Since she and Gage were dressed like hunters about to head out on a mission, no one would give them a second look, either. Everything was working as she'd hoped. Now if her racing heart would just settle down.

"They'll track us once we leave," Curtis said. His voice broke at the end. Fear was definitely getting to him. He must have gotten too nervous waiting alone in the garage. "As soon as they figure out what's happening, they'll be on our trail."

She shoved him out of the way and ducked her head under the dash. It took her less than sixty seconds to disable the GPS tracker. Piece of freaking cake. "They won't track you now."

She popped her head up and found Gage staring down at her.

And didn't the wolf look all solemn and determined?

"We'll come back for him," Gage promised her. "We'll get Jonah out, too."

She blinked. Okay, she hadn't been expecting that promise form him.

"Your brother's safe. He doesn't realize what Lyle is yet, so the shifter isn't going after him."

Curtis had run off and was punching in security codes, trying to get the gates open. And since no one knew he was supposed to be dead, he was schmoozing his way past the other hunters who'd just appeared. Feeding them some BS line about how he was off on another mission. The hunters were buying every word he fed them, and they were all just seconds away from a clean escape.

An escape that didn't include Jonah.

No.

"When Lyle finds out that I've escaped, he'll turn on my brother." She knew it. "I can't leave him behind." She wouldn't. She'd freed Gage's wolves. Done her part. Now they could get out of there. She and Jonah, well, they'd find a way out, too.

I won't leave my brother. Not even for Gage.

Gage lowered his head. "Yes, I figured you'd say something like that." His voice was calm. Huh. Weird. She'd thought he would fight with her. Do something. The wolves in the back were dead quiet.

She stepped away from the SUV. "Go." She cleared her throat. "When this is over—" Kayla stopped, not sure what to say. When this was over, she'd—what? She'd find her hubby and they could live happily ever after? That wasn't the way things worked. A hunter and a wolf didn't have a shot at forever. Besides, she wasn't even sure he wanted to stay bound to her.

Kayla pulled in a deep breath. So maybe she wouldn't offer any lines about what would happen when this mess was over. She squared her shoulders and told him, "Go take care of your pack." Then Kayla turned her back on him. Dammit, was she actually tearing up? What in the hell was happening to her? She was a fountain these days.

She took one step, then found her body hauled back against Gage's rock-hard chest. "Before I found you in that cage, I made a side trip by the infirmary." His breath whispered over her ear.

Kayla tried to jerk free. *No give.* "Gage?" Now she was afraid because his low voice had been so angry. So determined.

"While all the medics were busy stitching up the wounded hunters, I borrowed a few supplies from their office," he growled the words.

Her heart seemed to stop even as a dark suspicion grew in her mind.

The heavy garage door was opening with a groan and shriek of metal. Curtis was rushing back toward them.

"Sorry, sweetheart, but I'm not risking you," Gage told her and shoved something sharp—a needle!—in her arm.

No. *Jonah!* She opened her mouth, but Gage put his hand over her lips, smothering her instinctive cry. Her feet kicked back at him. Landed a hit. Another. But he didn't let her go.

And she could already feel the drug slipping through her system. First her brother, now Gage? Why was everyone drugging her? Such sonsofbitches.

"When you wake up, you'll be safe."

And he'd be a dead man.

Jonah. Her eyelids fell closed, and a tear slipped down her cheek.

Chapter Eight

She was still out.

Gage paced beside the bed, shooting frowns at Kayla's unconscious form. Just how long was the woman gonna stay that way? They'd gotten away from the compound. Made it back to the safe houses he'd set up for the wolves.

He'd met with his aides. Gotten extra guards to start patrolling.

And she was still out.

Had he drugged her too much? He put a knee on the bed and leaned over her. She was breathing okay. His hand lowered to her chest. Her heartbeat was good. Steady. No, um, actually, it was picking up now and—

Her eyelids flew open. She kicked out at him and landed an attack right to his groin.

Sonofabitch.

"Tell me you weren't groping me while I slept!" Kayla yelled.

He sucked in a breath. Well, at least she was awake, and she seemed very, very aware. No gradual waking for her. Just slam-bam, wake-up, ma'am. "No, I was...just...checking your heartbeat." He'd been too worried for a grope. But now that she was awake—

Her eyes narrowed. "Where the hell am I?"

Awake and enraged. He'd try to play things cool, for a while. "You're in a shifter safe house."

"Oh, hell, no." She jumped from the bed and rushed to the door. "This place might be safe for you, but I'm not a shifter. I'm a hunter. That puts me at the top of any shifter's kill list."

He caught her arm. Stopped her before she could race into the hallway. "You're my wife. None of my wolves would dare to hurt you." Or he'd tear them apart. Simple fact of pack life.

Her breath huffed out. "Yes, well, what about me hurting them?"

"You won't." Because she wasn't a cold-blooded hunter, out to destroy every shifter she saw. She'd never been like that.

Her shoulders fell. "I am so mad at you."

His aching cock attested to that fact.

"And I *am* going back for my brother."

Yes, he'd been rather afraid she'd say that.

"Those hunters—they all have to learn the truth, Gage. When they realize what Lyle is, they'll fight him. I know they will."

She had an optimistic side. He hadn't noticed it before. The optimism was cute. Kind of.

He freed her hand. Stared down at her and had to tell her, "Your brother's gone."

Her face drained of color. "What do you mean?"

"When Curtis came back to the SUV, he told me the guards had already reported your brother as missing. Even before we left the compound, he'd already broken out." He kept his voice flat as he delivered the news she had to hear.

She'd been so worried about leaving her brother, but—

He left you.

He didn't say the words. There was no need. She'd understand.

Now Kayla was the one who grabbed his hand. Her nails dug into his skin. "Find him for me."

Uh, he had enough problems of his own to handle. A pack to protect. A traitor to smoke out. A wife to woo.

Her dumbass of a brother could wait a bit.

"You *owe* me, wolf." Kayla's voice rose a notch. "You drugged me, you clawed my brother...now you *find* him." She licked her lips, then whispered, "Please."

Hell. Like he could resist when she stared at him with those big, lost, golden eyes. She looked so sweet and innocent, but she'd shot a man less than six hours before.

"Wolves are the best trackers out there," Kayla added. Damned straight they were. "You can get his scent. You can find Jonah for me."

She seemed to be missing the point. So he had to say, "What if he doesn't want to be found?"

Her lashes lowered. "I need to make sure...Lyle is so good at lying...what if Jonah didn't leave? What if he died?" Pain broke in her voice.

Gage nodded, then realized she couldn't see the movement. "I'll find him." He had to be careful. If he didn't watch it, the woman would realize just how much control she had over him.

Too much.

"But you have to help me find someone else first." Because he needed her just as much as she needed him.

A small furrow appeared between her brows as she glanced back up at him. "Who?"

"The mangy wolf who sold out my pack." He'd rounded up all the men and women in the Vegas pack. A pack he'd assembled.

Wolves on their own didn't survive. They needed the strength of a family. The security of a pack. Without a pack?

Hello, insanity.

There was a reason most serial killers were actually wolf shifters. They couldn't control their beasts. Not when they were on their own.

Hell, just look at what had happened to Lyle. The guy was grade-A psychotic, with no pack in sight.

The wolves needed the bond of a pack. Or the bonds of a mate.

Mated wolves never lost their minds. They never went down that slippery slope that led to the total darkness of the beast.

I won't go now, thanks to her.

Hell, yeah, he owed Kayla. She had no idea how much. When this battle was all over, he'd make sure he paid his debt.

"I didn't even know there was a wolf giving intel to Lyle —" Kayla began, but he cut through her words.

"You know now," he said simply. They both knew for certain now. "You can help me find the SOB. And stop him."

"Uh, yeah, I do have my awesome days," she stated with a roll of her eyes. "But I'm not psychic. I can't just magically tell you which wolf has been selling you out."

"Sweetheart, we don't need magic." Because he'd

already narrowed the field down to two wolves. The two that he'd trusted the most in the pack.

Those two wolves were being held in lockdown. Contained, away from the others.

His two closest friends.

One would be dying soon.

"Come with me," he told her and offered his hand. "Because I don't want to kill the wrong wolf."

She stared at his hand. Hesitated.

Come with me. He wanted her at his side.

"Fine," she growled, almost sounding like a wolf, "but if I'm gonna be in a den of shifters, you'd better give me my gun back."

He almost smiled. Such a bloodthirsty little hunter.

* * *

LYLE STARED out at the desert. It just stretched as far as he could see. Appearing empty. Almost never-ending.

The hunters were scrambling behind him. Trying to secure the facility.

The facility could burn for all he cared. He was tired of it all. He just wanted to shift. To run. To kill.

The quiet kills in secret weren't good enough anymore. Why should he have to hide? Act like he was something else?

The power was growing within him. The beast wanted *out*.

He'd come to this city, planning to take over. The place had been ripe. He'd been ready. No longer just taking orders from dicks in suits, he'd been set to change the game. To show them the real face of the paranormals they needed to fear.

Sin City had been meant to become his. He'd set his little dominoes up, then gotten ready to watch them fall.

Only Gage Riley was in his way.

He'll fall.

Lyle would make sure of it.

His weapon in this world was his gift at deceit. His mother had been right. He really had been born to lie. He'd fooled the hunters so easily. Would keep fooling them. They were his tools, and he'd bleed them until they were dry.

Then, once the other wolves were gone from Vegas, once the city was his, he'd let his wolf out. He'd let his beast rage, and he'd tear and claw his way through any hunters who were still left standing.

He wasn't a fucking lap dog. Not anymore. He was an alpha.

Time the rest of the world bowed to him.

Psychotic? Insane? Those words had been tossed around plenty by his parents. They'd seen him for what he was long before anyone else did.

So he'd stopped them from seeing. From hearing. From breathing.

Wolf shifters were supposed to maintain their control and balance if they lived in a pack. If they took a mate.

He'd thought about living in a pack once.

Even almost taken a mate.

But he'd had more fun killing her than anything else. Kayla's mother had sure been blessed with one sweet scream.

Mates and packs weren't for him. He didn't want the rigid bonds of control that would hold his wolf in check. He liked the blood. He liked the violence.

The desert stared back at him.

He liked the kill.

* * *

THE WOLVES WERE CHAINED to the wall. Chained with silver. Oh, jeez—who'd been the unlucky shifter who'd drawn that duty?

Kayla walked silently into the darkened room with Gage. Her gun was tucked into the waistband of her pants. Hell, yes, she'd gotten it back. Like she was gonna just walk into this room unarmed? She still wore the black hunter's uniform she'd taken before the big escape from the facility. Not like she had a lot of clothing options.

She didn't really know how Gage thought he'd be able to use her, but—wow. Damn, that one shifter was smoking. Smoke literally rose from the blisters on the blond man's wrist where he was bound.

Two shifters. One blond and fair. One dark, dangerous.

They'd been at the cabin. When Gage had first brought her to the desert, these wolves had been there. Like she would have forgotten them so soon.

I've narrowed it down to two. Now she knew what Gage had meant.

"Since you said there was no tracking device on you," Gage said as he crossed his arms and stared down at the wolves, "that means the hunters found us in the desert by another means."

A traitor.

"I didn't sell you out!" The blond wolf jerked against his chains. More smoke plumed in the air. The blond should know that the more he struggled, the more he'd burn. "Dammit, trust me, Gage!"

"That's the problem, Davis," Gage replied quietly. "I did trust you."

Kayla's gaze darted between the wolf shifters.

"Just as I trusted you, Billy." Gage's gaze swung to the silent, glaring wolf. The intense and dangerous one. "I trusted you both. With my life and the lives of the pack."

Only his pack members were under attack. Two had been taken.

Where were Shamus and Faye now?

Gage studied the two chained shifters. "Only two wolves knew that Kayla and I took shelter at that cabin. *Just you fucking two.*" Rage snapped through his words.

The dark-haired wolf, Billy, still wasn't talking. He just sat there, the silver chaining him, and glared back up at Gage with narrowed eyes.

"I've been with you for five years," Davis shouted, spittle flying from his mouth. "Do you really think I'd betray you to a human?"

"No." Gage spoke so instantly that Davis relaxed. The blond started to look confident.

But Billy quickly shook his head, obviously thinking the blame was coming his way. "No way, alpha, it wasn't—"

"I think," Gage said, cutting through Billy's words and still staring right at Davis, "that you'd betray me to a wolf."

Had Davis tensed at that charge? Yes, he had. His hands were straining against the cuffs. The shifter was desperate to break free. Not that Kayla blamed him. If she were burning, she'd be feeling pretty desperate, too.

But just how strong were the bonds on Davis? If another one of his pack mates had chained him, would that individual have felt some sympathy for the shifter? Maybe not tightened the silver chains enough?

"A wolf?" Billy asked, frowning. "What the hell are you talking about?"

Kayla stepped forward. Gage had brought her in there, so she figured it was time she did her part. "Lyle McKennis, the leader of the hunters...He's actually a wolf shifter."

Billy started to laugh. "You're shitting me."

"No, I'm not." Carefully, she studied the chained wolves. Davis had widened his eyes and the blond *looked* surprised. But his hands were still twisting within the bonds.

"And you knew?" Billy threw at her. "You knew what he was and you were still working for him?"

"I didn't know. I thought he was human." She'd been blind. Only seeing what she wanted to see. And was that why Gage had brought her in? Did he think he was blind where these two wolves were concerned?

She could understand that fear. When you trusted someone so much, it was easy for the person to mislead you. To lie right to your face.

But this time, things were different. It wasn't just about blind faith. Because this time, Kayla had a way to help Gage. After all, this really was her area of expertise. "Lyle's sent other operatives undercover in packs before." He liked to do that. Divide and conquer, that was his strategy.

"Like he sent you?" Davis demanded. His hands stilled as he looked up at her. "He just tossed you right at the big boss."

"I've been working with Lyle for years, so he didn't track me like he does others under his charge." No, when Gage had first asked her about a tracking device, she'd immediately denied having one. But, actually, years before, Lyle had implanted one just under her right shoulder.

She'd dug it out. She wasn't a dog to be tracked. Not even by the man she'd put up on a stupid pedestal.

And he sure did fall.

So Lyle checked in with her via regular calls. He didn't use the calls with his other hunters. That would have been too risky. Or so he said. He'd given her special privileges because she'd been his top hunter.

So he'd said. *Lying asshole.*

"They all have trackers," she whispered. "All the other hunters. In case they're ever captured or for when they find a target so they can be located easily." The better to apprehend the prey they'd caught. The better to send in the team for retrieval.

Just like the team that had come for her and Gage.

The chained men frowned at her. The silence in the room seemed heavy. Too thick.

"And you *don't* have a tracker, Kayla?" Gage asked, voice deep and rumbling as he broke through that silence.

She shook her head. But, hell, maybe that wasn't good enough. She pulled over the neck of her shirt, revealing the thin scar that sliced around her shoulder. "I took it out two years ago."

She'd thought it would be hard to figure out which member of the pack was betraying Gage. Checking *all* the pack for trackers? She didn't see that going over real well. Like they'd all be willing to strip for a hunter and let her search their bodies.

But with just two men, finding the tracking device would be a piece of cake.

"Who has it?" Kayla asked as her gaze darted between Davis and Billy.

"Search me all you want, sweet thing," Billy invited, his

slight accent thickening. "Strip me. Feel me up. I don't have anything to hide."

Davis lunged away from the wall—and his hands were free. Tricky wolf, he *had* been breaking out of his bonds.

But she'd suspected that. She dodged when he came at her, slicing with his claws. Kayla hit the floor and missed the claws that could have cut her open. Davis twisted and tried to come at her again.

But Gage had him. He caught the other shifter's hands and held them above Davis's head.

"You sold us out!" Gage snarled.

But Davis just laughed. "So the fuck did you. You're the one screwing a hunter."

Kayla grabbed the silver chain that had fallen behind Davis. "No, he's not just screwing me." She wanted to set that record straight. "He *married* me." She slammed the chain into Davis's side and watched him fall, howling. "So don't forget that!"

Then she turned to the other wolf. Billy. He was watching her with a slight grin on his face.

The silver.

Okay, if he was innocent, then it was time to free him. She rushed to him and started jerking on the chains.

"If Gage hadn't married you," Billy said as his grin widened a bit more, "then I would've. I love it when a woman kicks ass. There's nothing sexier."

The door opened. More wolves came rushing in. Wolves and that enhanced hearing of theirs. She guessed the guards outside had heard everything.

One shifter—a woman with short red hair—tossed Kayla a pair of keys. While Kayla went to work on Billy's chains, the other wolves closed in around Davis.

This wasn't gonna be pretty. Shifter battles never were.

"Why?" She heard Gage demand. "Why would you turn on your pack? You let them take Shamus and Faye. You let them take our own damn family."

Because to the wolves, pack was family. A bond that went even deeper than blood.

"They're not my family. They're strays. Strays that didn't belong in *my* pack."

Shamus shoved through the crowd of wolves. His claws were out and his face twisted with his fury. It took three other wolves to hold Shamus back when he went for Davis's throat.

Free now, Billy stalked to Gage's side. Good. He was showing that he stood with the alpha. Even if the alpha had ordered him chained.

"You were a stray, too," Gage fired, voice lethal. "We all were. That's why we came together. To be more. To be stronger."

"With you at the lead." Davis's lips turned up in a sneer. "Because you think you're the only damn alpha around."

"And you thought you could take me?"

"When the time was right, I fucking was!"

The right time..."When was that gonna be?" Kayla askcd, her own body tight with fury. "When you'd let the hunters take out all the other wolves? When you thought no one would come to Gage's aid? When you thought he was gonna be weak?"

"And I would be strong!" Davis yelled.

More growls from the wolves.

Kayla caught sight of Faye. Faye's claws were out. She wanted her pound of flesh, too. From the look on the shifters' faces, they all did.

Did Davis realize just how screwed he was?

"You think that you're strong?" Gage challenged as he yanked off his shirt and tossed it to the ground. "Then come and see if you can take me out. Fight *me*."

Oh, damn. She'd heard of this before. When one wolf turned on the others in his group, the shifter would have to face—

"Trial by pack," Billy said grimly.

Gage nodded. "Damn straight." Gage stared at the wolf who'd betrayed him. "And I'm going to rip you apart."

Kayla felt a shiver go down her spine. These men and women—right then, they were all barely human. She could feel the rage and wildness in the air. The wolves wanted out. They wanted to rip and tear and kill.

The line between human and beast was blurring.

"Here. Fucking now," Gage blasted.

The other wolves stepped back. Formed a circle around Gage and Davis.

Um, here? *Now?*

Gage began to shift. No wonder he'd tossed his shirt aside.

"I *should've* been alpha," Davis shouted. His eyes were wild. Shining too brightly. "I'm stronger. Smarter. You've been in my way for years." His bones popped.

Broke.

She hated the sound of shifting wolves. The growls. The pain.

The fury.

"It'll be over soon," Billy told her. His shoulder brushed against hers. He seemed to be trying to comfort her, when he'd been the one caged moments before. "Gage doesn't play with his prey."

That was supposed to make her feel better?

Kayla glanced around the room. She saw claws and lengthening canines everywhere she turned. It looked like every wolf there—except Faye—was about to shift.

And Kayla remembered another time. Another place. *A big black wolf, one that came at her with his fangs bared.*

Gage had finished his shift. He stood in the middle of that snarling circle. Big, strong, dark. His body vibrated with fury as he bared his fangs.

Her mother had still been alive. Broken, bloody, but breathing.

Davis had shifted. His coat was white. His eyes burning so brightly. He pushed down with his hind legs, then leapt at Gage.

She shook her mother. Begged her to get up. Then heard the growl.

A growl broke from Gage's beast. He swiped out with his claws, and blood spilled on Davis's white coat.

"First blood," Billy said, excitement thick in his voice. "Alpha always gets first blood. Hell, yes!"

The wolf had sprung at Kayla from the shadows. She'd tried to run, and his claws had raked down her back. She'd slammed into the floor, and he'd been on top of her. His mouth had gone for her throat.

The white wolf leapt up and sank his teeth into Gage's throat.

Then the door had opened. She'd told Jonah to wait outside. When they'd first arrived back at the house, something had been wrong. She'd known it. Because she'd heard her mother cry out for help. And she'd smelled the blood when she'd stepped onto the back porch.

Jonah had said that he'd wait outside for her. Jonah had promised. She'd made him promise.

Gage shook off the other beast. More blood flowed. The shifters in the room were shouting. Lifting their clawed fingers up as they cheered.

Cheering for death?

He'd broken his promise. Jonah had come in. Had she screamed? She couldn't remember. Would never remember, but she thought...she thought she had. She'd screamed and he'd come to help her.

Gage slammed his body into Davis's. They both hit the floor. Didn't get up.

The wolf had attacked her brother. Biting and clawing and Jonah had screamed. She'd been crying. Begging the wolf to stop.

"Stop," Kayla whispered.

The black wolf's head jerked toward her. In that wild stare, was there any of Gage actually left? *Only the beast.*

But when he turned to look at her, Davis used that moment to attack. His claws sank into Gage's shoulder.

Gage howled, and the memories blurred in her mind. "You can't distract him," Billy growled to her as his arms wrapped around her, and he pulled her back. She didn't even remember stepping forward. "He needs to kill the bastard."

Killing...that was all she'd known since that long ago night.

She'd managed to get to the drawers near the kitchen sink. She'd crawled her way there. Kayla had yanked open the top drawer and grabbed one of the knives inside. "Get away from him!" Her yell had distracted the wolf. He'd let go of Jonah.

Gage knocked the other beast away. Attacked again. Again. More blood. More howls. Gage was definitely stronger, but Davis was a dirtier fighter. And Davis wasn't giving up, no matter how much blood soaked his white coat.

The wolf came at her. She screamed and thrust the knife out. The silver handle glinted in the light before it sank into the beast's thick fur. The wolf stared at her, eyes burning bright, then leapt away.

With that knife still in him, he'd run through the open door.

Gage had his teeth at Davis's throat now. No more cheering calls came from the wolves. Only silence filled the room.

Like the kind of silence she'd known when the wolf left her alone in the house that reeked of death.

Her mother hadn't been moving. Her brother—he'd been so broken. Eyes shut, barely breathing. All because of a wolf.

"Stay with me, Jonah! Stay!" Her hands had grabbed him. Shook him. "It's gonna be all right!"

Her father was due home soon. He'd get there. He'd take care of them all. Everything would be all right.

Gage wasn't ripping Davis's throat out. Why not?

Her breath burned in her lungs. She didn't want to watch this anymore. She'd never wanted to watch.

Couldn't she have more than blood and death? Just once?

She turned away and pulled from Billy's arms.

She'd managed to drag and stumble her way into the living room. She'd grabbed the phone so that she could dial nine-one-one, then, there, in the corner, she'd seen—

Her father had already made it home.

"What the hell is the alpha doing?" Billy asked, voice whisper soft. "He can't let him live."

Kayla glanced back. Gage was shifting. Muscles and

bones reshaping. The fur seemed to melt from his flesh. Golden, strong flesh.

Davis was on the floor. Bleeding. Chest heaving. But not fighting, not anymore.

The shifters—at least a dozen, maybe two—were muttering. Glancing around uneasily. But they weren't attacking. For the moment, no one was.

"You wanted to join Lyle," Gage snarled and his voice was still closer to that of a beast's than a man's. "Then you fucking will. I'll deliver you to him and the hunters." His hands clenched. Hands now, not the paws of a beast. "From this moment on, you're out of this pack. Banished. If any one of us ever sees you again, *you're dead.*"

Gage wasn't killing Davis? He wasn't going to rip the other shifter open in front of the pack?

"You're Lyle's bitch, so he can cut you up himself. And I'm sure he will." Gage turned away from the wolf. "You're not worth my claws."

Billy whistled. "That is cold."

Gage's eyes were on her now. He was stalking toward her. Naked. Powerful. He...hadn't killed. Wolves killed. It was what they did.

She knew all about the pack trials. Two wolves. They fought until death. Only, this time, neither wolf was dead.

"I'm more than you think," Gage gritted out, and she barely could hear the words. Barely—because her attention wasn't on him in that instant.

It was on the beast behind him. The wolf that was now up, not looking nearly so injured. Up—and launching at Gage's back.

Kayla didn't waste time on a scream or a warning. Billy was already charging for Gage. He slammed into Gage, knocking the alpha out of the way.

But Davis wasn't stopping. He charged for both Gage and Billy.

Enough.

Kayla yanked out her gun. Aimed in an instant, and fired.

Chapter Nine

Because Davis had jumped into the air, the bullet slammed into the middle of the wolf 's chest. He fell to the floor and landed with a thud.

Gage tossed Billy aside. No one spoke. No one moved. No one, but Kayla.

"I guess that ends the trial." She lowered her weapon. Gage heard no emotion in her voice. And she was so pale.

Kayla's gaze swept the room. "Any other pack problems we need to solve?" Her tone implied there had damn well better not be any.

The wolves glanced his way. They had a dead wolf on the floor, one who'd died by a hunter's hand. Not exactly the way a trial by pack was supposed to end.

Gage looked back at Davis's body. Such a waste. And why? Power? Why hadn't the guy understood? Being alpha was a pain in the ass most days.

You had to put the pack first, when you wanted something for yourself.

I want her. A hunter, mated to a wolf.

You had to turn on your friends, even lock them up when necessary.

Billy wasn't meeting his gaze. Hell. How was he supposed to soothe that one over? A little, "Oh, sorry, man, I thought you were setting me up to die," wasn't gonna cut it.

And you had to lie to the woman you'd claimed as your wife.

Your brother's missing. No. Jonah wasn't. That line had been pure bull. Jonah was right where he was supposed to be—at Lyle's side. But Gage had to keep her away from that compound. He couldn't let her race back there. So he'd lied.

I'll save her brother. I'll make everything okay.

Davis's eyes were closed. The silver bullet had lodged in his heart.

The bastard had been his friend. "See you in hell," Gage muttered. Funny. He'd always thought he'd get there long before Davis did.

"Get rid of the body," he told Shamus. The redheaded wolf was glaring down at Davis's form. Yeah, after all that had happened to him, Shamus sure as hell wasn't taking betrayal well.

I don't take it well, either.

Neither did Kayla. So he was gonna have to be real careful how he played this next scene.

Except she was turning away. She kept her grip on her gun and she walked toward the door. The other wolves eased back for her, clearing the path.

Alpha.

They might not like her, but they respected her. Bullets and death had a way of showing a woman's spirit. No wolf within, but the lady was one hell of a fighter.

She killed to keep me safe.

And he hadn't killed because he wanted her to see him as more than a beast. More than a monster.

Could she even truly see him that way?

"Kayla!" Gage hadn't meant to roar her name so much as just say it, but the beast was too close to the surface for much control.

She stilled and looked back at him. She had a "don't-try-me" expression tightening her face.

He held out his hand to her. Some things had to be done.

For the pack.

For me.

Just in case something happened in the next battle, Kayla had to be protected. Her safety was what mattered.

"My wife." Now these words were softer, but still growled. It was time to claim his mate in front of the pack. She wasn't a hunter anymore. She was one of them.

Forever.

Confusion swept over her features. She glanced at the other wolves. Then back at him.

Gage kept his hand up. The pack needed to see them as unified.

Kayla licked her lips and took a step toward him. "Uh, Gage?"

Shamus hauled the body out of the room. Left a trail of blood in his wake.

Yeah, wolf pack life wasn't exactly sunshine and paradise, but his Kayla wasn't the sunshine type.

He didn't speak again, just waited for her to come to him. And she did. With slow, uncertain steps, when she wasn't the type for uncertainty, either. Her hand lifted and, hesitantly, her fingers curled around his. "What, ah, what am I supposed to be doing?"

She'd taken his hand. And he'd take her. "This," he said simply, then pulled her against him. His lips found hers in a hot, hard, openmouthed kiss.

The pack cheered around him. Blood, sex, and violence —yes, they all understood those three things.

He kissed her harder. His tongue tasted her. So good. The best he'd ever had.

Never let go. No matter what happened. No matter what he had to give up, Gage wasn't letting Kayla go.

And that was why he'd married her. Not for the pack. Not to get intel on her boss. Not even because she *might* be able to give him children since her scent marked her as a genetic match for a shifter.

He'd just wanted her. So he'd taken her.

His head lifted. Her lips were swollen. Red. "Mine," he said simply.

No one spoke.

Kayla glanced around. "Um...mine?" Kyla pointed at Gage's chest.

The shifters roared their approval.

She winced.

Damn but she was cute.

Gage lifted her into his arms. She was all that mattered. She might not realize it, but he'd pledged his life to her with that one simple word.

Mine.

Mine to protect. To care for.

Mine to put above all others.

Some of the pack might be pissed over Davis's death. Some wouldn't think that a human should have been involved in the trial. Some might even be wanting her blood.

Not anymore.

With that one word, he'd given a warning. Any who touched her would regret it because...

Mine.

No one hurt what was his.

Gage carried her from the room that smelled of death and blood, and he didn't look back.

* * *

WHEN THE BEDROOM door closed behind them, Kayla knew just what Gage had planned.

Not like it would take a genius to figure this one out.

"Gage, I need to find—"

He kissed her. Lowered her feet to the floor, then pushed her back against the wall. Her wolf was aroused, no doubt about it. And, okay, maybe she was, too. Gage certainly knew how to kiss.

Hell, yes, he did. Adrenaline still spiked in her blood, making her heart beat faster and letting that wild heat inside of her surge ever hotter but...

She pulled her mouth from his and sucked in a fortifying breath. "We have to—"

"Fuck," Gage finished, voice guttural. "I *need* you." His eyes blazed down at her. So bright. She loved the blue of his eyes. "Not about the pack. Not about hunters. I just *need you.*"

Her breath seemed to freeze in her lungs. Wasn't that what she'd always longed for? Someone who needed her? Someone who just wanted her, exactly as she was? Darkness, scars, and all?

His hands tightened around her arms. "I didn't marry you because you might be able to give me children."

That whole mate thing again. It could make a woman tense.

"I married you because I couldn't breathe without tasting you."

Oh, well. She wasn't even sure what to say to that, but his words sure made her feel good.

Besides, it didn't matter that she couldn't toss out a ready comeback. Gage didn't give her a chance to respond. He kissed her again. His aroused cock pressed against her. Long, full, so thick.

Why did I marry him?

Not for the mission. Not because he was a job.

Because I wanted him.

She still did. Always would.

So she didn't push him away. Why couldn't she have what she wanted? Couldn't she just take it? Take him? Her clothes were seriously in the way.

Her hands wrapped around Gage's powerful, broad shoulders, and she pulled him closer. She loved the way he kissed. The slow thrust of his tongue. The sensual press of his lips. She got wet just from his kiss.

His hands slid down her body. Curved around her ass. Lifted her up against his cock.

Yes.

Her body was already eager for him. She rubbed against him and liked it when he tensed against her. Power. It could come in so many forms.

His mouth lifted from hers. He stared into her eyes. "I'm not letting you go."

He wasn't talking about that moment. She got that part. But she didn't want to think about the future. About what could happen or who could tear them apart.

Then he was kissing her neck and she could just moan and shudder because, oh, *yes*, that part of her body was sensitive. When he used the edge of his teeth in the lightest of caresses, her eyes closed and her tight nipples pushed into his chest.

"Bed," he muttered against her. "I want—"

Her eyes opened. "No." Because this was also about what she wanted. Her hand pushed against his chest. That wonderful, naked chest and all those fabulous muscles.

Her sex clenched in eager anticipation. Soon he'd be thrusting deep and hard into her, but first, Kayla had other plans.

He was naked. His thick cock pushed up toward her. So she wrapped her hands around the aroused length that she craved. Stroked him. Pumped once. Twice. He swelled even more beneath her fingers.

Her mouth had gone dry. She wanted to taste him.

Kayla eased onto her knees.

"Sweetheart, you don't have to do this."

She put her mouth on him. That move shut up her wolf. Gage's eyes seemed to roll back into his head. She licked him. Sucked him. Loved his taste.

Her hands wrapped around the base of his cock as she took him into her mouth. Deeper. *Deeper.* She tasted him with each caress of her lips and tongue. Salty, wild. He tasted just the way she'd thought he would.

His hands were slammed against the wall now. Not on her. Gage wasn't trying to guide her movements or force her to take more of him. No. He was staring down at her with feral eyes. His claws were out—*in* that wall. And a ragged groan that was her name tore from his lips.

She smiled up at him, then took him deeper.

"Kayla."

She wanted him to come so she could taste every single bit of him.

His claws ripped from the wood. He grabbed her. She started to flinch away. His claws—

"Never...hurt you." His voice was barely human.

And he wasn't hurting her. He was yanking her clothes off, tossing them aside, and pretty much shredding the material with his claws, but he *wasn't* hurting her.

Then he was lifting her against the wall. His claws never even skimmed her skin. He lifted her up and parted her legs.

Kayla guided his cock to her core. When he thrust, she arched toward him so that his dick sank deep within her. *Yes.*

Their eyes locked. She couldn't look away from him. There was so much intensity in his stare.

Her sex clenched around his cock. Thrust. Withdraw. Thrust.

Kayla's hands locked around his shoulders as she rose up and then slid down, pushing back against him. She wasn't going to be able to hold back for long. She was too aroused. Slick, sensitive, her body greedily clutched him with every driving thrust of his cock. Again and again and again.

She opened her mouth. *Screamed* his name. Kayla didn't care who heard her.

Then he came inside of her. A hot rush of release that just sent the pleasure crashing over her again. She held onto Gage, digging her nails into his flesh. Marking him because no matter what the hell else happened between them, there was one thing that she was sure of. One absolute thing.

Mine.

Gage belonged to her.

* * *

New clothes were brought to them. A good thing, because the ripped look wouldn't have worked so well for Kayla. She dressed quickly and tried to peek at Gage's ass only three times.

Four.

Clearing her throat, she turned away. "I need to talk with the demon." Curtis might be able to tell her more about what had happened to her brother. She'd drill him, then start a search plan.

If her brother had left the compound, that meant he'd realized the truth about Lyle. He'd known she wasn't lying. He believed her.

"I'm afraid that's not gonna be possible."

Frowning, she glanced back over her shoulder. Gage was dressed now. No more sexy peeks at his ass. Pity. "Why not?"

"Because I had two of my pack escort Curtis to a safe location."

Her eyebrows rose. She'd thought they were already in a safe house. "Then escort me to this same location." Seemed simple enough to her.

But Gage didn't exactly look agreeable as he said, "I didn't want the demon knowing where I'd hidden the rest of the pack, so I didn't let him get close."

Right, okay, sounded fine to her. "He probably had a tracker on him anyway." Unless he'd dug it out. Without Lyle knowing? Maybe. The demon seemed to have plenty of secrets. "I would have mentioned that tracker bit to you," she muttered and some nice, remembered fury spiked her blood. "But you know, you *drugged* me first."

His lips tightened.

Speaking of trackers…"We need to check Davis's body. If he was tagged, then Lyle could already be on his way here."

Gage didn't look particularly worried about that scenario. "Yes," he agreed slowly, with a faint nod. "He could be."

Just like that, the light finally dawned. "You want him here." Gage wanted Lyle to come after them.

Gage held her gaze. "I dug the tracker out of the demon before I let him go to the safe house."

So he *hadn't* been so clueless after all. Tricky wolf.

"And I brought it here with me."

What? Her breath expelled in a rush.

"So I figure with the demon's tracker and Davis's both giving off a signal to this place, we'll be having company soon."

The killing kind of company. "Why?" Why would he want to bring the hunters to him?

"I brought in reinforcements." Gage shrugged and didn't even look a little bit concerned about the coming attack. "Wolves from other packs. Wolves who are tired of being hunted."

She couldn't read his expression. Nothing showed past the stoic wall of determination that hardened his strong features. "You're setting your own trap."

"It was my turn."

Or had it been his plan all along? Suspicion slipped through her.

"Shamus will be coming soon. He's going to make sure you're taken away from this place during the battle."

Was Gage saying she couldn't handle a fight? What? Did she *look* like a piece of fluff? "I've been battling since I was sixteen years old," she pointed out.

"So aren't you due for a break?"

She blinked at him, then forced her clenched jaw to relax. They'd gone from hot sex straight to him kicking her out? That was too fast of a one-eighty for her. "I'm not going to leave you when you need me." That was *not* who she was.

His lips tightened. "And I don't want you to see what I do to the hunters you once considered friends."

Her heart was about to slam through her chest. "You're not killing them all." That wasn't an option. "They think they're making the world a better place! That they're out there fighting monsters!"

"Then they should be prepared for when the monsters fight back."

She shook her head. No, no, she wouldn't let a bloodbath happen on her watch. "They only thought they were taking out killers. We had files, reports! We didn't attack innocents!"

But he just stared back at her, and her words seemed so hollow to her own ears. Nausea rolled through her. So many lies. Lyle had fooled them too well.

They'd let themselves be fooled.

"He's the one who should be stopped," she muttered and refused to back down. "The others—give them a chance, Gage."

"So they can fill my heart with silver? Cut off my head?" His smile held a cruel edge. "Sorry, sweetheart, that's not happening, not even for you."

A light rap sounded at the door.

Gage's nostrils flared. "Shamus."

"I don't want you to lose your damn head." She didn't move. She could still *feel* Gage inside her. She wasn't walking away and leaving him to a bloody battle. This was more than sex. Gage had better realize that fact.

"I won't. I'm rather attached to my head."

He was driving her crazy. "This isn't a joke!" She tried to keep her voice calm and make the wolf see reason. "The hunters will come in expecting a trap. Lyle will be ready to use and lose them all, if he can take you out." Because she'd seen the fury in Lyle's eyes. He wasn't stopping, not until he'd taken over this town.

And if he had to kill a few dozen humans and wolves? So what? He could always recruit more hunters, and he sure didn't care about the wolves.

"There's another way," she said, desperate. "There's always another way."

Gage shook his head. "There's no time." His steps were slow as he stalked toward her. His hand lifted and the back of his fingers slid down her cheek. "The wolf is at the door, and I'm gonna tear him apart."

Or he'd get torn apart. The humans would die.

This didn't have to happen. "What about my brother?"

Gage looked at the door. "We'll find him when the fight's over." Then his hand dropped. He marched away from her. Opened the door.

The redheaded wolf waited, with his arms loose at his sides.

"Take her back home, Shamus," Gage directed.

Home?

The thought was so foreign to her that Kayla blinked at first. But, she did have a home. An apartment in the city. One that gave her a night-time view of the strip that took her breath away.

So why didn't that place feel like *home?*

She took a deep breath and straightened her spine.

"Sorry, Shamus," she said—and then she slammed the door shut in the shifter's face.

Gage blinked. He looked surprised. Really? Had he truly thought she'd just follow meekly along to his plan? Not happening.

Kayla jabbed her finger in his chest. "I don't walk away from fights. Not ever. I don't tuck my tail between my legs and run—"

His brows shot up. Whoops, okay, wolf reference. Her bad.

Kayla cleared her throat. "I don't run because things get tough, got it?"

"This isn't—"

She jabbed him harder. "You don't get to spout 'mine' bullshit one minute and then toss me out the next." And it hurt. To go from the best sex ever to a cold toss out the door, yes, that was tough. But she wasn't about to let him see her pain. She'd never let anyone see.

Only Jonah.

Where are you, Jonah?

"Those men don't deserve death, and I'm not letting you claw your way through humans because a psychotic wolf has been jerking us all around." Kayla took another deep breath. Weren't deep breaths supposed to calm down fury? She wasn't feeling calm. "I'm working with you, and we'll make sure we take out the real monster."

There was still no emotion showing on his handsome face. "Just how are we gonna do that?" Gage wanted to know.

Yes, how the hell were they gonna do that? Plans and options spun through her mind. *Think.* "When the hunters come, don't send any wolves out. Not a single one." This was crazy, she knew it but crazy just might work. "I'm the only one who will face them. I'll make them see reason."

"Uh, sweetheart, no one believed you before."

Good point.

"You broke out of your cell. You ran from them." His lips tightened. "Those assholes will just shoot first and dump your body later. No dice."

He reached for the doorknob again. Yanked open the door.

Shamus was still there. One red brow was up. With his shifter hearing, a closed door would not have stopped him from eavesdropping on their little conversation.

There had to be a way of stopping this hell. She just had to show the others what Lyle really was.

But Lyle wouldn't be in that first wild rush of hunters who came to storm the place. He always held back. Gave the orders from a distance. Moved in when the targets were secure.

When the hunters attacked, they'd be out for blood. *Mine.* Dammit, yes. And Gage's. So to save all their sorry asses, one dark options sprang to mind. "We have to attack first."

Shamus whistled. "Bloodthirsty. I like that."

Gage punched him.

"They're coming after us. Getting ready. Moving out." Kayla was talking faster now because she *had this.* "So this is the time when we go for them. We attack while they're en route. We close in on Lyle, we take him out of the caravan." When heading into new territory, the hunters swept in on a straight line. "The last SUV." That was his. *Always.* "We take him out, and we make the others see what he is."

They'd drag his sorry ass out of that SUV. Tie him in

silver. When he started to burn, the other hunters would be forced to see him for what he truly was.

"And you think that's gonna stop them?" Gage demanded, his voice full of doubt. "They'll just shoot him and then keep coming after my pack."

Because hunters hated wolves. They thought shifters were monsters that needed to be put down.

It was Kayla's turn to shake her head. "We're not all like that." *I'm not.* She needed him to recognize that truth in her eyes. "Give us a chance to show you that we can be more." *Better. I can be better.* Not just a lost soul seeking justice for crimes long ago. A woman now, wanting to fight for the man she was craving more than life.

Slowly, very slowly, Gage nodded. "But if this doesn't work...if they keep attacking..." He lifted his claw-tipped hands. "They will be stopped."

And she knew what he really meant was...they will be dead.

* * *

Gage paced down the hallway with Shamus. Kayla was arming herself. Getting bullets. The silver that the pack handled only with reinforced gloves.

She was hot when she got battle ready.

She was also dangerous.

"Hunt for me," Gage told Shamus, because no one in the pack hunted like the red wolf.

Shamus gave a slight nod. "The prey?"

"Her brother."

Surprise flickered briefly over Shamus's face. "You want me to kill him?"

"No." If he did that, he'd lose her. "I want you to make

148

sure his fool ass stays alive." Gage yanked out a scrap of cloth he'd taken from the compound. Cloth that had once been Kayla's shirt. "His blood's on this." When it came to humans, Shamus could track a scent with deadly accuracy. "Take him out of the fight."

Because Jonah would be coming, Gage had no doubt about that. Coming for his sister and coming for vengeance.

Shamus took the cloth. Turned. Walked quickly away.

"You can't lie to her."

Billy's voice. Coming from a few feet behind him. But then, he'd known Billy was there, watching.

Slowly, Gage turned to face the wolf he'd considered his friend. The burns from the silver had faded. Mostly. "I'm sorry." For the pain Billy had suffered.

Billy lifted one shoulder in a shrug. "You're alpha. You do what the hell you want."

Not when it meant that he hurt the ones he cared about. So he tried to explain, even though an alpha wasn't supposed to justify. *Just act. Rule. Dominate.* There was more to Gage than that, though, there always had been. "Only you and Davis knew Kayla and I were at that cabin. And you two were both close with the other wolves who went missing." It was easier to be lured out into the open, easier to be attacked, when the one luring you wore the guise of a friend.

Shamus had told him that both Davis and Billy were near the site when he was taken. He'd broken away from them and attacked the hunters. Been trapped, but the other two had both gotten away.

And when Faye had gone missing, they'd been there, too. Been there, but hadn't managed to save her.

"So you shackled me in silver." Billy exhaled and glanced away. "Damn painful, hoss. Damn painful."

For the pack. "The silver wasn't about pain. It was to make sure neither of you ran before I could find the real traitor."

Billy peered back up at him. "You could have *asked* me first."

Asked him. Asked Davis. One wolf would have lied, and no matter what the stories said, Gage wasn't the sort of wolf who could actually smell a lie.

He didn't think those beasts existed.

So Gage just stared back at Billy. "Davis wanted you to look guilty." He'd been setting the other wolf up all along. Timing their guard duty together, even tossing seeds of suspicion out among the pack. "He planned to let you take the fall."

"Yes, I figured that. The bastard probably thought he'd kill me." Billy's claws flashed out. "But I'm tough to kill."

So others had discovered. There was far more to the shifter than met the eye. He'd run from his home in the South because he'd wanted a fresh start.

But Gage knew what he'd left behind. The death and hell that waited in the South was one of the reasons he'd suspected Billy.

"We can't run forever," Gage warned. It was a lesson they all needed to learn. Maybe it was time for Billy to face his own demons.

Time for them all to face that darkness.

Gage kept his hands by his side. "You want to charge at me, come the fuck on." Billy deserved his pound of flesh. The first slice would be free. After that, Gage would slice back.

Billy shook his head. His claws were out, but he made no move to attack. "I don't like fuckin' silver." He turned away. "But I like this pack. Pack first. *Always.*"

Gage knew that Billy understood. The pain didn't matter. Not when there was a pack to protect.

"Next time, *ask*," Billy snarled over his shoulder.

Before the wolf could storm away, Gage grabbed his arm. "I will." He exhaled a rough breath. "And for now, right now, I'm *asking* you to help me."

Billy's brows shot up as he looked back at Gage.

"We're going after Lyle. Taking out the last SUV that comes onto our land because Kayla says he'll be in that one." Minimum bloodshed. Right. He knew that was what she wanted. Wolves—well, they liked the blood.

A lot.

But for her, he'd try.

"I want a scent blocker." It would be the only way they could sneak up on Lyle. Lyle couldn't know they were closing in if he couldn't smell them. "I know you've got a stash." Another reason he'd suspected Billy. "Get it."

The shifter nodded and rushed away.

Gage watched him go. He'd try it Kayla's way, for a time. He'd give the orders for all of the other wolves to stand down. But if her plan didn't work, if one of those hunters fired at them first, then the wolves would be the ones to finish the battle that the humans had started.

Chapter Ten

The SUVs slid onto the old, broken road just after midnight. The vehicles crept forward in a long, snaking line, with their headlights off and their engines barely growling, just as Kayla had predicted.

"Now I know why you picked this place," Kayla whispered from beside him. "One way in, one way out."

Damn straight. He'd laid his trap so carefully. The hunters had miles to go before they were even close to the safe houses he'd set up for the pack. And they didn't know it, but the hunters were already surrounded by the wolves.

Easy kills.

"That's him." Kayla pointed to the last SUV. One a bit bigger than the others. "That's the one Lyle always uses."

Because he liked to send the others in first. Gage knew the bastard was a coward at heart. Why else would he send humans to do the dirty work for him?

"Come on." He grabbed her hand and headed into the darkness. The goal was to separate that lat SUV from the others, but they wouldn't have much time. The hunters were the shoot-first variety, and he'd already told Kayla what would happen if some trigger-happy dick fired at him or her.

Death.

He had a wolf stationed nearby, one who knew to take out the last SUV as soon as Gage gave the signal. The guy wasn't just a shifter, though. He was one grade A, first-class sniper. Gage waited, wanting that SUV closer. *Closer.*

He lifted his hand. In the dark, humans couldn't see so well.

Wolves could.

There was no thunder when the weapon fired, but the SUV's front left tire blew out. Then the right tire exploded. The SUV swerved, flipped, and thudded into the earth.

And Gage and Kayla were already moving. Racing toward the wreckage even as the other SUV drivers slammed onto their brakes.

Hurry. Hurry.

Gage punched his fist through the already broken passenger side. He yanked open the door, nearly ripping it away from the vehicle.

Lyle hadn't been driving or waiting in the passenger seat, but the bleeding bastard was slumped in the back of the vehicle. Gage pushed past the two groaning men in the front and grabbed his prey.

"Judgment time, asshole," he snarled. Then he kicked out at the back doors of the SUV, knocking them wide open, and he hauled out that sorry excuse for a wolf.

Blood poured from a gash on Lyle's forehead. He was bleeding, but laughing. "Y-you're...dead," Lyle gasped out. *"Dead!"*

"No," Kayla said, voice clear in the night. Footsteps thudded, coming close. The other hunters were swarming. "You are," Kayla told him.

Then Gage heard the snick of a gun. *One shot*. That was all it would take.

The pack would attack.

Kayla whirled around and used her body as a shield to block Gage and Lyle. *"Stand down!"* she screamed. "Or we'll all die!"

Not her. The others, yes, but Kayla wasn't leaving him. He wouldn't let her go.

He could see the hunters now. Three were already close enough for him to kill easily. Gage could leap forward and slice their throats in seconds. Did they honestly think the guns in their hands made them stronger? Fools.

"Let him go," one of the hunters ordered from behind his black ski mask. Masks. These bastards were always hiding. And they said shifters were the ones who pretended to be something they weren't.

"He's been lying to you all," Kayla cried. Wait, hold the hell up. Had she just put her weapon down?

Kayla lifted her empty hands in the air.

She fucking did.

Gage growled.

Lyle shouted, "Shoot her!"

Gage slapped his hand over the bastard's mouth. "No matter what else happens here tonight," he promised softly into Lyle's ear. "I'm cutting you open."

Lyle heaved in his hold, but Gage was stronger. He just tightened his grip around the jerk.

"No one has to die tonight," Kayla said, proving, quite clearly, that a human's hearing was nothing compared to a shifter's. "I've worked with you all—so many times—just give me a chance to prove that what I'm saying is true!"

They weren't lowering their weapons. "Move back, Kayla," he ordered. Because his wolves were going to spring up soon, and he wanted her away from the coming bloodbath.

"Let him go," the guy at the front of the growing pile of hunters snapped. "Let Lyle go, then we can talk."

Such a lie. Once Lyle was clear, the hunters would open fire. They were holding back only because Gage was a claw away from killing their precious leader.

"If Gage lets him go," Kayla replied, "Lyle will kill me." After the briefest of pauses, she told them, "Then he'll watch while you all die, too."

The hunters shifted restlessly, from one foot to the other.

"Don't you wonder why he's never touched silver?" Kayla questioned them. "Why he always uses his black gloves when he's near the silver cells?" Kayla shook her head. "You've seen all this, just as I have. Only I didn't put the pieces together. I didn't want to believe he was the real monster."

The tension in the air thickened.

He didn't like this. Every muscle in Gage's body was battle ready. The hunters hadn't fired yet, but Kayla's small body had no cover if the bullets were to start raining on her.

Too vulnerable. Standing in front of him, offering herself up to the hunters. Hell, no, this wasn't acceptable.

He heard the faint snap of a twig. To his left. Gage inhaled and pulled in the scents around him.

"I can prove what he really is," Kayla promised her voice clear and loud for all to hear. "I can—"

Gage leapt toward her. Lyle broke from him as he moved, rolling to the ground. Gage didn't even look back at that prick. He grabbed Kayla even as the thunder of a gun echoed around them.

First shot.

Now it would be his turn to attack, and all the bastards would die.

The bullet blasted near him, scraping over his arm and ripping open the skin. Gage didn't cry out. He was too long acquainted with pain for that. He twisted his body and took the impact when he and Kayla slammed into the earth.

Then he opened his mouth and roared the order, "Kill!"

The wolves had already shifted. They were ready. Eager for the fight to come.

The foolish hunters wouldn't have a chance.

"*No!*" Kayla shouted, but it was too late. He'd given the order.

Streaks of black, gray, and white burst from the darkness and lunged for the hunters. The humans were trying to fire, but they couldn't aim well at their targets. Not in the dark. Not with so many wolves rushing around them and moving so quickly.

"It doesn't have to be like this," Kayla whispered, then she shoved away from Gage. "It *won't* be like this."

She ran right into the battle.

Dammit, *no.*

His claws burst out of his fingers as he took off after her. Lyle had raced to a nearby SUV. Big surprise, he was trying to jump inside and make a run for it. A coward to his core.

"Going someplace?" Kayla demanded, then she grabbed a gun right out of the hand of a nearby hunter. She slugged the guy, and he fell to the ground with a thud.

Nice punch. That right hook was really killer.

Kayla aimed the gun at Lyle. "Get away from the vehicle. Get your ass out here right now, shifter!"

Two hunters jumped in front of Gage. He could have just slit their throats with one long swipe of his claws.

He knocked them out instead. Just slammed their heads together and stepped over them when they fell.

Another hunter was rushing up behind Kayla. Why were they all in their damn ski masks? Why—

Too close.

Gage leapt to take out the man sneaking up to attack Kayla but a gun blasted and, in the next breath, a bullet slammed into Gage's upper back.

Sonofabitch.

The bullet went through right under his shoulder and tore out the front of his body. Snarling at the pain, Gage whirled around. He saw the hunter just steps away. The prick giving off the heavy scent of fear and sweat. The bastard with the shaking hands. And the gun that was about to fire again.

"Bad mistake," Gage told him. Then he attacked. His claws cut deep into the fool's wrist. The gun clattered to the ground—and the hunter fell, too, crying and begging for mercy.

Mercy? What the fuck did he look like?

Kayla screamed.

Gage whirled back around. A hunter had her in his arms. Held tight against his chest. The masked man had a gun.

No. Not her. *"Kayla!"* Gage's roar thundered over the gunshots and the howls of the beasts around him.

"Shoot her!" Lyle screamed. He was hanging with his body half-in, half-out of the SUV. Lyle's hand was rising. He'd gone into that SUV to get something.

A weapon?

Kayla slammed her head into the hunter's face, driving against the ski mask that covered his features. Then she jabbed her elbow into his side and kicked down hard on his foot.

The hunter's hold eased on her. She moved, spinning around, and knocked the gun from his grip even as she put that hunter down on his ass.

Gage had never seen a better alpha female. *Never.*

He ran toward her, grabbed her, and pulled her close. "I fucking love you."

Her gasp filled his ears.

Then, because Gage knew what was coming and he didn't have time to do anything but protect the woman he loved, Gage twisted his body to shield her.

And when the bullet hit him—the bullet that had been fired from the gun clutched in Lyle's white-knuckled fist—Gage felt the burn of the silver in every inch of his body.

"Gage!" Kayla's scream. Her hands were on him, nails digging into his chest.

He tried to fight through the burning agony. Kayla wasn't safe. Lyle would shoot at her again. The bastard had to be stopped.

The beast was coming out.

Gage lifted his hand and saw that the shift had already started. He hadn't even felt the break and snap of his bones, but his hand—*not the hand of a man.*

Kayla lifted up her gun and fired at Lyle. Again and again. "Shift," she commanded Gage. "*Shift!*"

The hunter she'd pounded was trying to lift himself off the ground.

And the shift was too damn slow. Kayla was battling Lyle on her own, and Gage tried to force his body to transform faster. But the silver was in his blood and every breath hurt.

Her bullets slammed into Lyle, but they weren't silver.

She'd grabbed a hunter's weapon, but the idiot hadn't packed silver. Why? Lyle's order? Had he *wanted* the humans to die?

When her bullets hit Lyle, the bastard just laughed as his blood flowed. And he took aim at Kayla again.

"No!" Not Gage's scream, because he couldn't scream in that moment. He could roar and howl, but speech was lost to him.

The desperate cry came from the hunter that Kayla had attacked and knocked down. He was lunging for her now, but Lyle had already fired his weapon.

Kayla leapt to the side. The bullet tore across her hip and the scent of her blood broke Gage and his wolf.

The shift finished in a white-hot burst of agony. The pain didn't matter. Kayla did. Gage leapt up and charged at Lyle. Lyle took aim on him then. Lyle's finger tightened around the trigger. His total focus was on Gage.

You want me, asshole? Gage snarled.

Lyle just kept smiling. Completely out of the SUV now, the sick freak stalked forward. Smiling, watching Gage, and aiming his gun.

The fool never saw the wolf closing in behind him. The wolf with a coat tinted red. The wolf who would want his own justice.

Shamus leapt at Lyle before he could fire again. His claws dug into Lyle's back as the red wolf took him down.

Lyle screamed.

The chaos around them seemed too quiet for a moment. Hunters spun around. They'd ignored gunshots, too immune to the sound, but Lyle's echoing scream of pain and rage—they hadn't ignored that.

Two men immediately fired at Shamus.

He jumped away from Lyle's bleeding body.

Lyle rolled clear of Shamus, then he managed to stagger to his feet. "K-kill—" Lyle began.

"No." It was the other hunter again. The one who kept going after Kayla. The one who was now holding her arm. Holding *her*.

Gage tensed. That scent...

The hunter jerked off his ski mask. *Jonah.* Her brother. "Everyone just—stop!" Jonah shouted.

The wolves weren't stopping. They were attacking. Killing.

The hunters fought back. No one was listening. Shamus was transforming slowly back into the form of a human. Lyle was trying to grab another weapon.

And more asshole hunters were attempting to get at Gage and Kayla.

Kill them all. They could end this now.

"Screw this!" Kayla's voice. So sweet and vicious. That was his lady. His head jerked around, and he saw her bend down. She grabbed a gun from the holster on Jonah's ankle. "Silver?" He heard her ask.

Jonah nodded.

Kayla lifted the weapon. Aimed it at Lyle. *"Silver!"* she screamed.

But even as she fired, two hunters pointed their weapons at her.

Gage took one of the pricks out with a slash of his claws across the guy's legs.

The other hunter—Jonah shot him in the arm.

And Kayla shot Lyle. Her bullet ripped into his chest. Lyle flew back and fell onto the ground. Smoke drifted up from his wound. Smoke...as the silver burned his flesh.

And the hunters were watching him. Every. Second.

"What the hell?"

"How the fuck...?"

Many stood now, lost, confused. It was the perfect time for the wolves to take out the humans. So easy. Like slaughtering sheep.

"Lyle is a wolf!" Kayla yelled. "He's been lying to us, tricking us all along!" Her voice seemed to echo in the night.

The men and women in their ski masks still had their weapons. But they weren't fighting. Not yet. Some were too injured to fight. The scent of blood was strong in the air. Some were too scared. A wolf always knew the scent of fear.

"Gage and his pack aren't evil." Kayla's voice was clear and strong. "They haven't done anything to the humans in this city."

Well, nothing that the humans hadn't asked for. The wolves weren't exactly perfect. No one was.

"We don't have to destroy each other!" Kayla's eyes burned with intensity, just like her voice. "We can just walk away from this fight."

If the hunters didn't start walking in less than five seconds, they wouldn't have a choice in the matter.

The wolves were standing back, for the moment, but it would just take one howl from Gage to send them into action. *Just one howl.*

Then Jonah strode forward. "We aren't killers." His words carried easily. There was a heavy edge of command in his words. "We protect. This *isn't* us."

Lyle was digging the silver out of his chest.

A few of the hunters lowered their weapons.

"A damn shifter? All along?"

A woman yanked off her ski mask. Her face was pale. Shaken. "What...what have we been doing?"

"Following the wrong path," Kayla answered with a sad shake of her head. "And it's time to change that. It's time for all of us to change and to make this right." She was at her brother's side. "Walk away from the wolves. These shifters aren't the ones who are evil." She swallowed, exhaled, and said, "To them, *we're* the evil ones. We're the ones who came after them when all they were doing was trying to live."

Silence.

The wolves were straining forward. So eager to finish the fight.

Gage didn't give the order to attack. Not yet.

"Put up your weapons. Clear out of here," Jonah said. His words held the unmistakable whip of an order. "This fight isn't ours." His gaze slanted back to Lyle. Still on the ground. Still clawing at his chest as he tried to dig out the silver. Disgust tightened his face. "And you sure as hell aren't our leader."

The rest of the hunters lowered their weapons. Then they slowly headed back to their vehicles.

No more fighting. Just...walking away?

Well, fuck me.

Kayla had been right. They weren't out to kill blindly. They weren't killing at all.

"I'm sorry," Gage heard Jonah say to Kayla. "I should have trusted you sooner. Hell, you're the only one I *should* ever trust."

Her hands reached for his.

Gage's eyes narrowed. *Get to her.* He raced toward them, his claws tearing over the earth.

Faster, faster.

"Everything's gonna be okay now," Jonah told her, and he pulled her close for a hug.

Gage opened his mouth and snarled.

Jonah jerked away from Kayla and saw Lyle—charging

right for them. Bleeding, but with the silver gone, the bastard wasn't done yet.

Not even close.

"This isn't how it ends!" Lyle screamed as spittle flew from his mouth. "Not for me!" His claws lifted. "Not for you!" He went for Jonah's throat.

Gage locked his teeth around Lyle's leg and jerked him back. He'd wanted his pound of flesh, and he *had* made a promise to the other wolf.

You're dying. A promise was a promise.

"This *is* how it ends," Kayla said as she backed up, pulling her brother with her. "So have fun in hell, asshole."

Lyle was shifting. Fighting. Clawing. "Your father—you know he begged to live!"

Kayla flinched.

"Begged!" Lyle spat. His face was elongating, his eyes burning bright. "So did your bitch of a mother—"

Gage slashed his throat.

The bastard stopped screaming.

You won't hurt her anymore.

The other wolves closed in.

And Lyle didn't scream again.

* * *

"Come back with me," Jonah said. The other hunters were long gone—headed back to base or to who the hell knew where.

Maybe some of them would just keep driving. Keep running.

Kayla didn't blame them. Everything they knew had all just changed. They had to figure out what they were going to do. Who they were going to become.

Lyle was dead. The wolves were shifting back to their human forms. Turning to their alpha for guidance.

"You don't belong with them," Jonah told her. Her brother was standing strong and steady beside her. His hand rested on her shoulder. "Come back with me. We can go forward."

"Forward to what?" she asked. When you were lost, how the hell did you know which direction to take?

His hand tightened on her. "Not everything was a lie. Lyle was working for the government. He was a contractor, yes, but he was being sent out after real killers. Those cases were real."

"Not all of them." And that knowledge would keep tearing her apart. "Some of those people that we captured were innocents, Jonah. Supernaturals that Lyle just framed because he wanted them under his control." Or because he'd just wanted to take them out.

"Then we free them," he vowed simply. With such determination. When had her kid brother grown up on her? "We find the containment areas that are housing them, and we make sure that they get their freedom."

She nodded. Yes, yes, that was what they had to do. No matter what it took, she had to give the ones she'd taken justice.

"We can do it," Jonah said, voice rough, eyes deep, "together."

Her gaze slipped away and found Gage. Surrounded by his wolves. Standing tall. Powerful. "He told me that you were...missing. That you'd disappeared from the compound."

Silence.

She didn't need Jonah to confirm the lie. She'd already figured it out on her own.

"He didn't want me to go back for you." Her shoulders sagged a bit. It had been one hell of a day. Week—*year*.

"It doesn't matter," Jonah returned without hesitation. "I was coming for *you*. I saw Lyle burn in that holding cell. I knew the truth, and I was coming to make sure you were safe."

No wonder he'd been stationed so close to Lyle.

"I figured it was my turn to stand guard," her brother told her softly.

She glanced back at him. Found his gaze on hers. He looked so worried.

"I'm sorry." His voice held a ragged edge. "Oh, damn, Kay, I'm so sorry for everything that happened. I *shot* you."

"With a tranq."

He looked away. "You're the only thing I care about in this world. The only thing that *kept* me in this world, when I was sure ready to leave it."

She'd known that. She'd seen his eyes. All those long days in the hospital. All the surgeries. All the pain.

It was her turn to reach out to him. "You'll make it up to me."

"Following orders," Jonah muttered and shook his head. "I'm not a damn robot, and it was *you*. I should have trusted you. Not listened to the lies about you falling for a wolf."

Gage's head snapped their way.

Ah, shifter hearing. His eyes narrowed on Jonah. Yep, that was a flash of fury in his gaze.

I fucking love you. His words whispered through her mind again.

So it hadn't been a candlelit confession. No roses and fancy dinner and sweet words. It had just been pure Gage. Heat of the moment. In the middle of the fight. Rough. Hard.

Her wolf.

"Let's get out of here," Jonah urged her. "The wolves should just be left alone."

Her eyes were on Gage. "I don't want to leave them alone."

Jonah stiffened. "Uh, what?"

Gage stalked toward her. He was wearing jeans now. Someone in the pack had brought backup clothing for everyone.

Prepared pack.

"I'm not going back," Kayla said. She'd always feared a wolf's claws. Hated the power of the beast. But Gage was different. His beast made her feel safe. He made her feel loved.

"Kayla, it was just a job!" Jonah sounded more than a little desperate. "Just a mission gone bad!"

"No." Gage was almost on them. Her words weren't really for Jonah anymore. They were for Gage. It was time for him to understand. "It wasn't just a mission for me."

"Aw, hell. " Jonah stepped back in surprise. "You did fall for the wolf."

Gage's gaze swept over Jonah. "You're healing."

"Yes, well, a slash to the arm can take some time to mend. Not like we all have magical healing powers."

"You're lucky I didn't kill you." Gage flashed his fangs. "You ever shoot at her again and I'll—"

"I'll be damned." Jonah's jaw dropped. He shook his head, and took a minute to recover before he said, "You love my sister."

Kayla frowned at him. Did he have to sound so shocked? Gage blinked and looked annoyed. Just the way she felt.

Gage said, "I married her, didn't I?"

It really was that simple. But she'd been too blind—too scared and desperate—to see the truth from the beginning. It wasn't about packs.

About mates.

About hunters.

It was just about them. Man and woman.

Need. Lust. Desire.

Love.

"But the real question is..." Gage's voice had deepened and his focus was on her. Totally. "Just why the hell did she marry me?"

The wolves were watching. Her brother stared with wide eyes.

Kayla didn't speak.

Jonah cleared his throat. "Um, see, man, there was this mission..."

Gage shoved her brother away. Shamus grabbed Jonah's arm before he could charge back at him.

"Was it just the mission?" Gage wanted to know. "Tell me, Kayla."

Kayla shook her head. He had to hear the mad galloping of her heart. The drumbeat filled her ears. So loud.

"Then why?"

So many eyes on them. *So many.* She knew how important this moment was. To the wolves. To her.

To Gage.

She lifted her right hand—and realized she was still holding the gun. Jonah's backup weapon. The one he kept loaded with silver.

She tucked it into her waistband and lifted her hand again.

"*Why?*" Gage demanded.

She smiled at him. The pain and horror of the past were

slipping away. Her hand touched Gage's strong chest. "Because you're mine, wolf."

She heard the growls of approval from the pack.

Mine.

"And I don't plan to ever let you go." The pack would need to get used to that fact. *Deal with it.* They'd have a hunter in their midst from now on.

She wasn't afraid of the big, kick-ass wolf. She loved him too much for fear.

Kayla pulled her wolf closer. Stood on her toes. And kissed him.

She'd promised forever at that little chapel, and forever was exactly what she'd give him. Wolves weren't the only ones who mated for life. Humans could sure as hell do that, too.

Forever.

Gage's arms closed around her, and Kayla knew that she was exactly where she was supposed to be. With the man who loved her.

She was home. At last.

Epilogue

THE BRIDE TOOK SLOW, DELIBERATE STEPS DOWN THE aisle. The officiant smiled at her, but he was sweating.

Hmmm. Was all that sweat due to the fact that he was in a building full of wolf shifters and hunters?

The hunters were on her side of the chapel. Looking fairly nice and presentable. No black ski masks. No weapons. They'd *better* not have brought weapons to her wedding.

The wolves were on the groom's side. Again, fairly nice and presentable. As long as you didn't look too closely. If you did, you might see the flash of some fangs. Maybe a few claws.

The groom waited at the end of the aisle. He wasn't smiling. He'd smiled before. On her first walk down the aisle. Back then, he'd looked so casual and open, but that cool appearance had been a lie.

There weren't going to be any additional lies between them. Not now. That was why they were starting over. This time, they were getting things right.

"You okay?" her brother murmured. Kayla turned her head and found Jonah watching her with worried eyes.

What? Did he think she was going to break and run? She was already married to the wolf. But Gage had insisted on another ceremony. One in front of the pack. One without any kind of deceit. One to tell their kids about.

Whatever. I'm telling the kiddos about the first marriage. And the wild ride of fighting and running that followed.

Because she never wanted to lose those memories.

"Kayla?" Now Jonah was paling. Probably because he was afraid he'd have to tangle with a little chapel full of big old wolves.

She smiled at him. "Everything's gonna be all right."

He exhaled on a slow breath. Then nodded.

Poor guy. He was getting used to the wolves now, slowly. The Vegas wolves had started working with the group of hunters that were left. They were all rescuing those unjustly imprisoned under Lyle's psychotic reign. And stopping the real supernatural threats that were still out there.

Having a wolf on your side could be a very, very good thing.

At the end of the aisle, Kayla stopped walking and stood in front of Gage. So strong. So dangerous. So hers.

A very good thing.

The official started talking. She was supposed to be listening. This was all important.

She couldn't hear anything but her own heartbeat. She couldn't look away from Gage's eyes.

Had wolves really haunted her nightmares for years? Because she couldn't imagine her life without this one wolf.

Then Jonah placed her hand on top of Gage's. She

repeated vows—for the second time. She pretty much had no idea what she said, but that didn't matter.

Because soon Gage was kissing her, and she was kissing him back. She had her forever, and it was the best thing in the world.

The best.

The wolves howled and the hunters cheered, and Kayla got her happy ending.

* * *

GAGE CARRIED her over the threshold. Not some too-pink honeymoon suite this time. But into his home. His bed.

Not that they were gonna make it that far...

Kayla was already stripping him.

He tried to slow her down. "Sweetheart, let's go slow, let's—" Gage hissed out a breath. Her hand was on his cock. He shuddered. Okay. Screw slow. They could do that one next time. They had nothing but time now.

They made it to the couch. He pulled off her dress— she'd been so beautiful in it—then stared at her white garter belt with desperate eyes.

"Um, Kayla?" His hand tightened on her thigh. "You weren't wearing any panties." Just that sexy as hell garter and thigh-high stockings. Hot enough to make a man drool.

She smiled. "I figured I'd save us a step."

And even though lust was freaking eating him alive, laughter burst from him.

Kayla. She'd gotten to him from the very first moment. Wrapped him around her little, lethal fingers.

He spread her legs. "Well, if it saves us a step, that's a damn good thing." He put his mouth on her. Licked and kissed her delicate core and grew even more frantic for her.

Love her taste.

Her hips arched against him. She was wet. Ready. But he wasn't done tasting.

His tongue slid into her. His thumb pushed over her clit.

She shivered beneath him. Her nails dug into his back, marking him. For a human, the woman sure had some strong she-wolf tendencies.

He stroked her again. Licked.

And felt the tightening of her muscles around him. That was it. Just a little more.

Kayla came against his mouth.

It was gonna be one hell of a night.

Gage used his teeth to pull down her stockings. He took his time licking and kissing her skin.

"Gage!"

Definite she-wolf tendencies.

He thrust into her. Sank as deep as he could go. It still wasn't deep enough. Would anything with her ever be enough?

He kissed her. Withdrew. Thrust. Her legs wrapped around him. Her arms held him tight.

Nothing else was this good. This perfect.

The beast inside was snarling. Wild for his mate, and his mate was wild for him.

Kayla's nails scratched down his back.

When she came again, he erupted within her seconds later. *Just the start.*

He'd make sure that the woman screamed with pleasure every day of her life. Every. Single. Day.

Gage wrapped his arms around her. After a while, he finally managed to get them to the bedroom. This time, he wouldn't have to worry about a silver knife being shoved at his heart in the middle of the night.

Kayla already had his heart. She didn't need to try and take it again. It was hers to keep, for the rest of their lives.

He lowered her onto the bed and stared down at the hunter who'd come for him. His wife.

No, there would be no silver knives this time. They *would* get a real honeymoon. And if they didn't, he just might have to kill someone.

Gage climbed into bed with her and pressed a kiss to Kayla's lips.

Forever had never tasted so good.

Want more paranormal romance? Check out MONSTER WITHOUT MERCY.

Anyone can be tempted…

Xavier Hollow is the king of destruction. A shifter, a vampire, a demon—every nightmare you have—all rolled into one very smoking hot package. Xavier snaps his fingers, and the world falls at his feet. His enemies tremble in fear. And the women who want him? They tremble with yearning. Life (and death) is one fabulous ride…until a certain very old curse kicks in for him. A curse that threatens to take away all of his dark power.

He needs someone good...to fall for him. STAT.

Three days. That's how long Xavier has to tempt one Mercy Josephine. Innocent, pure, the actual descendant of an angel, she's all the things that normally give him hives—literally. He's allergic to good and just can't stand it. Committing a "good" act causes Xavier physical pain. The bigger the act, the more intense his suffering. But, for Mercy, he'll have to pretend to be someone very, very different. Someone who is—unfortunately and ever-so-disgustingly—good.

He'll corrupt her. She'll save him.

A simple enough task. Go to the costume ball. Charm the modern-day princess. Get her to sacrifice her soul for him. *Done.* He could probably bring her to the dark side with just a kiss. But then he meets Mercy and realizes that he's not the only one looking to destroy some goodness. Other beasts are closing in, and in order to break the curse that haunts him, Xavier will have to do the one thing he never expected...protect Mercy. Beautiful, brave, and—shudder— *good* Mercy.

The plan won't change.

By the time the clock strikes midnight on the third day, Mercy will be under his spell. He'll convince her that he's a hero, that she's desperately in love with him. She'll give up her soul—and her life—for him. The desire that rages between them is hotter than the fires of—well, home. Temptation is his specialty, and he can seduce her like no other.

Not like he's going to change his mind for her. Not like…

Not like anyone can teach a monster to love. Because only the good love. And Xavier is many things, but he will never, ever be good. Not when being bad is so much fun.

Time for the world to burn. Time for an innocent to fall. And time for the monsters to reign…

MONSTER WITHOUT MERCY is a steamy paranormal romance (41,000 words) featuring one seriously intense hero, lots of life-or-death drama, and more monsters than you can handle. HEA guaranteed and no cliff-hangers.

Author's Note

Thank you so much for taking the time to read Wed or Dead! I've always enjoyed writing about paranormal characters. Anything can happen in the pages of a paranormal book, and that *anything* is what makes the stories such fun.

I was thrilled to have the opportunity to rerelease Wed or Dead. I loved the idea of two opposites seriously attracting... your mate is the person who should be your enemy. Drama!

Again, thank you for reading this paranormal story.

If you have time, please consider leaving a review. Reviews help readers to discover new books—and authors certainly appreciate them!

If you'd like to stay updated on my releases and sales, please join my newsletter list. (I give all new subscribers a free Cynthia Eden book!)

I'm also active on social media. You can find me on Instagram and Facebook.

Best,

Cynthia Eden

cynthiaeden.com

More Books By Cynthia Eden

Protector & Defender Romance

- When He Protects

Ice Breaker Cold Case Romance

- Frozen In Ice (Book 1)
- Falling For The Ice Queen (Book 2)
- Ice Cold Saint (Book 3)
- Touched By Ice (Book 4)
- Trapped In Ice (Book 5)
- Forged From Ice (Book 6)
- Buried Under Ice (Book 7)
- Ice Cold Kiss (Book 8)
- Locked In Ice (Book 9)
- Savage Ice (Book 10)
- Brutal Ice (Book 11)

Wilde Ways

- Protecting Piper (Book 1)
- Guarding Gwen (Book 2)
- Before Ben (Book 3)

- The Heart You Break (Book 4)
- Fighting For Her (Book 5)
- Ghost Of A Chance (Book 6)
- Crossing The Line (Book 7)
- Counting On Cole (Book 8)
- Chase After Me (Book 9)
- Say I Do (Book 10)
- Roman Will Fall (Book 11)
- The One Who Got Away (Book 12)
- Pretend You Want Me (Book 13)
- Cross My Heart (Book 14)
- The Bodyguard Next Door (Book 15)
- Ex Marks The Perfect Spot (Book 16)
- The Thief Who Loved Me (Book 17)

The Fallen Series
- Angel Of Darkness (Book 1)
- Angel Betrayed (Book 2)
- Angel In Chains (Book 3)
- Avenging Angel (Book 4)

Wilde Ways: Gone Rogue
- How To Protect A Princess (Book 1)
- How To Heal A Heartbreak (Book 2)
- How To Con A Crime Boss (Book 3)

Night Watch Paranormal Romance
- Hunt Me Down (Book 1)
- Slay My Name (Book 2)
- Face Your Demon (Book 3)

Trouble For Hire
- No Escape From War (Book 1)

- Don't Play With Odin (Book 2)
- Jinx, You're It (Book 3)
- Remember Ramsey (Book 4)

Death and Moonlight Mystery
- Step Into My Web (Book 1)
- Save Me From The Dark (Book 2)

Phoenix Fury
- Hot Enough To Burn (Book 1)
- Slow Burn (Book 2)
- Burn It Down (Book 3)

Dark Sins
- Don't Trust A Killer (Book 1)
- Don't Love A Liar (Book 2)

Lazarus Rising
- Never Let Go (Book One)
- Keep Me Close (Book Two)
- Stay With Me (Book Three)
- Run To Me (Book Four)
- Lie Close To Me (Book Five)
- Hold On Tight (Book Six)

Bad Things
- The Devil In Disguise (Book 1)
- On The Prowl (Book 2)
- Undead Or Alive (Book 3)
- Broken Angel (Book 4)
- Heart Of Stone (Book 5)
- Tempted By Fate (Book 6)
- Wicked And Wild (Book 7)

- Saint Or Sinner (Book 8)

Bite Series
- Forbidden Bite (Bite Book 1)
- Mating Bite (Bite Book 2)

Blood and Moonlight Series
- Bite The Dust (Book 1)
- Better Off Undead (Book 2)
- Bitter Blood (Book 3)

Mine Series
- Mine To Take (Book 1)
- Mine To Keep (Book 2)
- Mine To Hold (Book 3)
- Mine To Crave (Book 4)
- Mine To Have (Book 5)
- Mine To Protect (Book 6)

Dark Obsession Series
- Watch Me (Book 1)
- Want Me (Book 2)
- Need Me (Book 3)
- Beware Of Me (Book 4)

Purgatory Series
- The Wolf Within (Book 1)
- Marked By The Vampire (Book 2)
- Charming The Beast (Book 3)
- Deal with the Devil (Book 4)

Bound Series
- Bound By Blood (Book 1)

- Bound In Darkness (Book 2)
- Bound In Sin (Book 3)
- Bound By The Night (Book 4)
- Bound in Death (Book 5)

Stand-Alone Romantic Suspense
- Waiting For Christmas
- Monster Without Mercy
- Kiss Me This Christmas
- It's A Wonderful Werewolf
- Never Cry Werewolf
- Immortal Danger
- Deck The Halls
- Come Back To Me
- Put A Spell On Me
- Never Gonna Happen
- One Hot Holiday
- Slay All Day
- Midnight Bite
- Secret Admirer
- Christmas With A Spy
- Femme Fatale
- Until Death
- Sinful Secrets
- First Taste of Darkness
- A Vampire's Christmas Carol

About the Author

Cynthia Eden loves romance books, chocolate, and going on semi-lazy adventures. She is a *New York Times*, *USA Today*, *Digital Book World*, and *IndieReader* best-seller. She writes romantic suspense, paranormal romance, and fun contemporary novels. You can find out more about her work at www.cynthiaeden.com.

If you want to stay updated on her new releases and books deals, be sure to join her newsletter group: cynthiaeden. com/newsletter.

www.ingramcontent.com/pod-product-compliance
Lightning Source LLC
Chambersburg PA
CBHW010751310726
48974CB00004B/881